EDISON AND THE DINOSAUR ZOO

N. R. MACKIE

www.dinosaurzoo.co.uk

Edison and the Dinosaur Zoo

It's not the dinosaurs that you need to be wary of
– it's the people!

Edison Hope's greatest dream has come true - he has been offered a job at the Dinosaur Zoo.

However a violent robbery inside the zoo sets in motion a series of events that puts Edison's teenage life in danger.

When a mysterious stranger starts to stalk him after a serious accident Edison has to make some life changing decisions.

How far will he go to protect his family, his job and the zoo?

A coming of age story, that builds to a dangerous and shocking conclusion.

Edison and the Dinosaur Zoo is the exciting debut novel by N.R. Mackie.

www.dinosaurzoo.co.uk

Thank you for your order
all the best – Nick

EDISON AND THE DINOSAUR ZOO

N. R. MACKIE

www.dinosaurzoo.co.uk

Edison and the Dinosaur Zoo

It's not the dinosaurs that you need to be wary of – it's the people!

Edison Hope's greatest dream has come true - he has been offered a job at the Dinosaur Zoo.

However a violent robbery inside the zoo sets in motion a series of events that puts Edison's teenage life in danger.

When a mysterious stranger starts to stalk him after a serious accident Edison has to make some life changing decisions.

How far will he go to protect his family, his job and the zoo?

A coming of age story, that builds to a dangerous and shocking conclusion.

Edison and the Dinosaur Zoo is the exciting debut novel by N.R. Mackie.

www.dinosaurzoo.co.uk

Edison and the Dinosaur Zoo

by

N.R. Mackie

First published by N.R. Mackie in 2012

Edition 2 (April 2012)

Visit the authors' blog at: www.dinosaurzoo.co.uk

Please feel free to email at: nick@shufti.co.uk

ISBN-13: 978-1475229202 (CreateSpace)

ISBN-10: 1475229208

This novel is a work of fiction. The names, characters and incidents portrayed are the work of the authors' imagination. Any resemblance to actual persons, living or dead, companies and events is entirely coincidental. As far as the author is aware no Dinosaur zoo actually exists.

Various drafts of this book has been registered with The Writers Guild of America (2009-2012) and ProtectRite (2011-2012)

For Kaja and Taro, with love.

Prologue.

The door at the bottom of the steps opened and slammed shut. The stranger must be coming up the stairs after him. He crouched down in the wet undergrowth and waited. He would try and surprise the man, a hard punch or kick might knock him over again, and then he could run back down the steps to escape. He heard the man's heavy breathing as he approached through the undergrowth. The stranger was furiously swishing something, possibly a stick, through the vegetation.

In the dark he could just make out some stars in the night sky, the storm clouds fading. They must be in one of the enclosures, he thought, thankfully this one seemed empty. He remained crouched down as he heard the man moving in his direction.

"Where are you, thief?" The stranger angrily shouted, getting nearer.

He sprang up and threw his strongest punch, and then a furious kick, in the man's direction, both connected. It felt like hitting concrete. The intruder momentarily stepped back, paused, and then with a furious roar launched himself at his assailant. He sensibly darted aside, jumped, and crashed down into the long grass. The huge stranger let out another angry roar, and in frustration started to swing his arms in blind punches, hoping to connect with his prey.

It was then that he caught sight of scores of little red eyes, illuminated in the dark, blinking behind his assailant. Built above the stairway was a rocky outcrop surrounded by bushes, and this was where the inquisitive eyes were starting to stir. They had disturbed and woken a cluster of sleeping creatures. It quickly dawned on him that they were indeed inside an enclosure, and that this one wasn't empty; this one had real, living dinosaurs in it!

"Oh shit." He whispered.

The tunnel they had just run down must have been for transporting the creatures between enclosures. It was one of the many private access conduits used by the keepers, enabling them to move dinosaurs and deliver food.

He hid as best he could and wondered what the hell he was going to do? He was trapped, with the huge pursuer directly in front of him and a mass of angry looking dinosaurs clumped around the only escape route. He didn't know much about the specifics of the different dinosaurs, but he knew well enough that most of them were vicious, with sharp teeth and claws, that would inflict a terrible bite. Some were even venomous, with poisons not unlike a snakes.

The air was suddenly filled with a high pitched yelping and hissing. The little creatures weren't very happy at having intruders in their territory. Their alarm call sounded urgent and spooky, bouncing around the enclosure, in the dark. He watched their tiny bright eyes, as they moved their heads about in a rhythmic wave. He could feel their hunger and keenness to attack.

He took the small torch out of his pocket, turned it on, and threw it in the direction of the stranger. It passed over the huge mans head and landed in a thud below the gang of dinosaurs, illuminating their reptilian bodies. The man turned as the torch passed by and came face to face with more than thirty snarling Segisaurus, each the size of a large domestic cat, huddled angrily on the rocks.

Caught off guard, the assailant stepped backwards, away from the tunnel entrance. One of the creatures launched itself off the rocky outcrop and jumped onto the man's solid shoulder. Immediately it sank its razor sharp teeth, into the man's thick muscular neck. He screamed in shock as the needle fangs penetrated his skin and instinctively brushed the creature off. The dinosaur landed on the ground next to his feet. The stranger began to violently stamp on its small splayed body, and he heard the sound of its bones snapping like brittle twigs. The creature's pitiful cries increased the agitation amongst the others in the pack, who watched from the safety of the rock face. The huge man rubbed at his neck where the creature had bitten him. He looked at the blood, now running down his neck, and staining his hand.

"Sod it!" The huge man shouted. He turned back towards the place that he had last seen his prey.

"Get out here, now!" He screamed. "Or you really are a dead man."

With his back now turned towards them the Segisaurus started to launch themselves off the rocks in small groups. They landed in huddles on top of the man's head, back, and shoulders. Their needle sharp teeth and long claws slashing at his skin. He could see bloody gashes appear on the man's face as he struggled to move away, with at least fifteen of the creatures attacking him. They viciously hung on to him as the huge man turned in circles using his flaying arms to try and prize them off. The man's cries chilled him to the core; he couldn't imagine the pain these creatures must be inflicting.

Now was his only chance. He sprang up, and in the darkness, ran frantically towards the escape door, past the mass of violent slashing and ripping. The screams of pain in the air propelling him along as he jumped down all of the steps and landed heavily against the wooden door. A sharp and painful jolt passed through his shoulder, but he couldn't stop now.

Quickly he pulled at the door, it wouldn't open. A bolt of pain, like an electric shock, shot through his hand. At first he thought that he must have touched one of the electric fences but then he looked down and yelled, a Segisaurus was hanging onto his arm by its teeth. He vigorously shook his body and thumped the creature hard against the door frame. The Segisaurus came flying off taking a chunk of his upper arm with it.

The small creatures were jumping and landing onto the ground around him. He didn't dare look down. Again he pulled frantically at the heavy door; conscious of the huge mans frantic screams behind him.

The door was locked.

Chapter 01
Edison and the Dinosaur Zoo.

Edison Hope had been too young to remember the first time that he visited the Dinosaur zoo. He knew that his Mum and Dad had still been together at the time, and that he had been just a baby. A faded family photograph of them all lovingly huddled together, inside the zoo, survived from that day. Edison is sitting up in his pushchair, flanked by his parents, huge smiles, outside a Stegosaurus enclosure. Whether any concrete memories of that day were still squirreled away in his brain, Edison couldn't be sure. In the photo his Dads face is blurred, he must have moved as the camera captured the moment. Edison kept the picture safe in his bedroom. It was hidden amongst his huge collection of dinosaur models, sitting under a large plastic Brontosaurus on a bookshelf. It was the only remaining image Edison had of his Dad before he vanished from their lives. Mandy, Edison's Mum, had destroyed or hidden all the others.

Edison was sitting high up in a leafy oak tree observing the world below. He waggled his legs against the heavy branch he was sat on and felt the sharp bark rub against his trousers and through to his skin below. A gentle breeze of fresh air brushed his perspiring face and cooled his scalp under his short chestnut coloured hair. He had climbed this tree many times before and instinctively knew which branches and footings to use to get high up into the canopy. His mind had mapped the geography of the inner tree and he climbed quickly, but methodically. His legs and arms had grown lean and powerful from his regular climbing. His hands tough and strong, past cuts and grazes to his fingers during climbs.

His position in the tree gave him an aerial, if distant, view of the city's Dinosaur zoo. The whole unique zoo and much of the City of Clifthill stretched out below him. Although not quite a teenager it was Edison's dream to one day work at the Dinosaur zoo. Perhaps even become a keeper. He had written regularly to enquire about the possibilities of getting one of the highly sought after weekend jobs, but he knew that he was too young.

Edison liked being high up in the tree. Up here he was safe to observe the world in total secrecy. No one could see him hidden, so high up, amongst the dense foliage. It was a huge ancient oak, probably older than the zoo itself, perched high on a grassy hill. He had spent many weekends and summer evenings here observing. The bird life he saw, the rustle of leaves, the distant cries of dinosaurs, the sirens of emergency vehicles way below in the city streets. Edison often took snacks and a drink along with him in his small green rucksack. He also had a notebook to draw in and jot down ideas. A small pair of binoculars was hidden inside an old squirrel dray in the trunk of the tree just above the branch where he sat. These were safely wrapped in a couple of plastic bags to keep out the weather. So far no one had discovered them. The world looked and sounded different from here, time almost stopped.

Today was the last day of the school holidays and Edison had decided to take a walk over to the city's large area of common land, opposite the zoo, where the oak tree stood. The walk from the modern block of housing-association flats where he lived, with his Mum and Step-Dad, took him down narrow leafy streets and past many grand Georgian townhouses. One of these houses belonged to his friend Orla Stone and her family. Edison and Orla often walked to school together, though she was a year older, and so in the year above him. Orla was funny, a little bit wild, and slightly taller than him. Edison had always had a crush on her, although she thought of him as the younger brother she never had.

"Hi Edison," Orla Stone hung out of a window as he had passed her house. Her freshly washed long hazel hair wrapped up in a bath towel.

Edison looked up and waved.

"Hi Orla."

"Wait there I'm coming down." Orla chirped.

He had hoped not to bump into Orla today. No one knew about his secret hideout and he hadn't told Orla. She wasn't the best at keeping secrets and loved gossip. If he told her about his tree it wouldn't remain a secret very long.

"Hello Eddie." Orla sang as she ran out of the front door.

"Hi Orla," Edison replied. "One of your cats has just escaped."

He pointed to the skinny, fur-less cat now climbing up the large wisteria bush running up the front of the house.

"No worries. It's just Kojak. She will climb back down again, probably." She said, adjusting her hair wrap.

They both watched as the cat carefully ascended the thick interlocked stems of the wisteria knocking off blue petals as it went. The cat seemed to be heading for the roof.

"She's always climbing." Orla explained. "You know Kojak is a girl don't you?"

Edison nodded yes.

"We couldn't think of any bald female celebrities to name her after." Orla shut the path gate. "All celebs wear wigs anyway, even the ones with hair."

Orla was the font of all knowledge, celebrity gossip, pop music, film star romances, she knew them all. Often she was completely wrong, but Edison let her get away with it. She lived at home with her mother, older sister and three expensive furless Sphynx cats. Her dad worked for most of the week in London.

"Dad doesn't do fur." Orla once told him. "So we got bald cats."

The cats looked weird without fur and had spooky eerie meows. They climbed everywhere and over everything. They had also been known to leave little smelly presents hidden behind the sofa, inside flowerpots, on Orla's bed, but rarely in their cat litter trays provided. Outside they tended to climb or get lost, going to the toilet alfresco was the last thing on their tiny fur-less minds. Edison thought that their toilet training was abysmal. He didn't have any pets, but if he did he wouldn't let them poo everywhere, especially inside the house!

"Where are you going?" Orla asked.

"Umm? Just to the shops, for Mum." Edison lied.

"Can I come?" Orla said excitedly.

Edison couldn't think of what to say. He liked Orla, a lot, but he still didn't want to tell her about his secret lookout. Suddenly a blanket of wisteria leaves fell down out of the air and Kojak the cat landed, with a bounce, onto the front lawn. It shrieked and hissed and ran around the garden.

"Kojak!"

Orla ran over to the stunned pinkie grey cat and scooped it up. She hurried to the front door.

"Sorry Ed. Kojak looks a bit shocked. He may need medical attention!"

Orla ran inside shouting "Mum? Dad? Kojak just fell off the roof!"

"Stupid bloody cat." Orla's Dad remarked from somewhere inside the house.

Edison guessed that the Stones must have their vet on speed dial.

#

Edison swept his binoculars across the vista before him and looked down at the zoo. It covered a reasonably large area and was enclosed by a tall stone wall.

Originally built as a traditional animal zoo in 1843, the area was surrounded by elegant houses and luxury flats. It was one of the wealthier parts of the City of Clifthill. The front entrance to the zoo ran parallel to 'The Downs', the city's spacious grassy common and parkland, where Edison now sat, watching from his tree.

He looked down at the numerous dinosaur enclosures surrounded as they were by secure fences, moats and ditches. 'Walters Tower', a tall stone folly stood centrally within the zoo. A warren of walkways, paths and narrow roads, both public and private, mapped themselves around the zoo. These joined the enclosures, gravel lines scoured into the landscape. From this vantage point the zoo looked like a model village, the huge buildings miniaturised and 'Lego' like. Edison could see the modern science block, the administration offices and the zoos eating area, 'Claws Cafe'. All looked to be made from some amazing kit. It reminded Edison of the small toy zoo he had at home with its replica buildings and plastic dinosaurs.

The zoo was at its busiest at weekends. He could see happy families eating picnics and ice creams. Groups of friends sat laughing on the grass. Children played in the activity areas, shimmying down monkey slides and diving onto dinosaur shaped bouncy inflatables. He saw noisy kids mucking about with their parents and though he couldn't hear their delight, from this distance, he could see the happy smiles on all of their faces. Sometimes this made Edison feel unhappy. His Mum couldn't afford to take him to the zoo and his Step-dad, Alex, was too mean.

Edison looked at his watch. It was approaching midday. On Saturdays the zoo would present one of it fantastic dinosaur displays. As often happened, the zoo rounded off the show with its flying pterodactyl routine. For this they used their most domesticated and tame pterodactyl, nicknamed 'Ted'. The pterodactyl had been hand reared by keepers when it had been a sickly youngster and rejected by its siblings. The adult Ted was about the size of a large macaw parrot and as domesticated as a prehistoric dinosaur could be.

The keepers would let Ted take off and fly around the perimeter of the zoos picnic area. The crowds were amazed as he circled just above their heads. Usually the pterodactyl stayed in the air and returned after a few rotations. Sometimes if he was feeling cheeky he stopped off and landed on the Cafe roof or in the picnic areas trees. This would cause great excitement, the crowds not knowing where Ted would land or what he would do next. More often than not he would swing upside down from the roof, hop off, and walk about a bit on the grass, before returning to the stage. The keepers had great faith in Ted returning safely to them, which he always did.

This particular sunny afternoon something must have spooked the creature and instead of doing his regular flight around the Dinosaur zoo he started to lift higher and higher into the air. Edison had seen the bright red beam of a laser pen being flashed around the zoo. Some idiot must have pointed it in the direction of the flying pterodactyl.

It was a warm day and Ted effortlessly used the thermal up-drafts to rise high into the air above the zoo, his rotations upward getting wider and wider. Edison couldn't hear the crowds down below in the Dinosaur zoo but guessed they must be gasping. The underside of the pterodactyl's wings flashed bluish silver in the sunlight. Edison followed it with his binoculars and realised that it was getting closer and closer to his tree. Its flight had taken the pterodactyl level to the tree on the hill, where Edison sat, amazed and now a little scared.

Edison lost sight of it as it travelled high above the top of the tree and out of view. He craned his neck, looking up through the dense canopy of leaves, trying to see where it went, but it was gone. Edison carefully relaxed his grip on the trees trunk and let out an audible gasp. He had never heard of one of the prehistoric creatures leaving the zoo before, let alone witnessing it! He wondered in what kind of panic the zoo keepers must be in right now and whether the story would be on tonight's local news.

Suddenly something crashed into the tree canopy just in front of him. The thick bushy leaves rustled and a few small branches cracked and fell to the ground below. The pterodactyl had landed into the tree only a few feet away from Edison. The creature hung upside down with its back to him and was using the tree as a vantage point to look down on the zoo. Edison held his breath and tried not to make a sound. He didn't want the creature to know that he was there. Though he had read that Ted was quite tame, he also knew that all pterodactyls had vicious beaks and claws. Edison didn't want to become its next meal. The creature was nearly as big as him and with its wings outstretched; much, much bigger. Edison had nothing to protect himself with, or to fight it off, if it did decide to attack.

the branch. The rough bark ate into the palms of his hands and he felt it cutting into his skin. He just couldn't grip hard enough to stay secure, his hands sliding. In a moment he was falling. He remembered crashing into snapping branches as he fell and watching the underside of the branch get further away. Though he tried there was nothing to grab onto and his arms waved helplessly in the air. As he fell he thought he could hear the crowd's relief and applause as the pterodactyl returned to the keepers in the zoo. He descended to the sounds of their distant cheers and clapping.

Edison felt himself hit the ground, hard. Even though he landed in long grass intense pain shot through his back. He let out a deep groan as all of the air in his body was smashed out of him. His head turned to one side and he thought he saw his lost binoculars but his eyes couldn't focus properly. It was at this point that Edison blacked out.

Chapter 02
The Letter.

"Give it to me Alex!" Edison yelled, as his Step-Dad dangled the envelope in front of his face, taunting him. He could see the Dinosaur logo stamped beside the postmark, meaning that the letter must be officially from the zoo. Edison had to see what was written inside as soon as possible. He had to get the letter.

Edison had returned home bruised and stiff from his fall, and didn't have the energy to fight with Alex. He had woken cold and confused at the base of the tree. How long had he been unconscious? He wasn't sure but his clothing felt damp and wet. The long grass and vegetation beneath the tree had helped to cushion his landing.

He had risen unsteadily to his feet and checked for any injuries. A few cuts, but remarkably he was fine considering the height of the fall. His arms and legs ached but it was his back that felt the worst. There was going to be a huge bruise there in the morning. He would have to be careful to keep the cuts and bruising secret from his Mum for the next few days. If she ever found out about his aerial acrobatics he was sure to get grounded.

Alex quickly pulled the letter away as Edison again made a grab for it.

"It's addressed to me!" Edison cried making another fruitless lunge. Alex stepped away and disdainfully dropped the letter to the ground. Edison stooped stiffly to pick it up as Alex used his boot to pin it to the carpet. The weight of the boot was creasing the envelope. Edison couldn't pull it out without damaging or ripping it.

"Say Please." Alex mocked.

Edison looked up into Step-dads big stupid face. Alex was at least two feet taller than him. Edison had grown to hate his thin sneering lips and bleached blond spiky haircut. Alex was a grown man, but he dressed like a gangly twenty year old Mod, or well dressed football hooligan.

"Please, Alex. May I have my letter?" Edison replied flatly.

"Have it," Alex took his foot away, "But you owe me."

Edison quickly picked it up and sat on his bed.

"It's just a stupid letter." Alex laughed.

"It's not stupid, it's from the zoo!" Edison cried. "And it's addressed to me!"

"Probably just another rejection letter, *Ed-weird*." Alex said sarcastically as he walked out of the room.

Edison really hated his Step-Dad and couldn't think what his Mum saw in him. Alex had lived with them for nearly two years now and Edison still hadn't grown to like him. The feeling was mutual, as Alex couldn't stand Edison either. Both tried to stay out of the others way but Alex couldn’t help but try and wind him up.

He took great pleasure in sneaking into Edison's room and deliberately breaking and hiding things. Edison had spent a long time lining up his plastic dinosaurs in different combinations and orders, such as large to small, the colours of the rainbow etc. Alex would move them about changing their order, thinking it funny. It annoyed Edison a lot, but complaining to his Mum wouldn't change things, sometimes it just made things worse. Once Alex had secretly taken a hack saw to three of the larger dinosaurs and cut them at their necks. He had then carefully balanced the decapitated heads back onto the bodies. When Edison came to play with them, the heads all dropped off.

Edison hopped off the bed and sat down in the old armchair he had squeezed into the corner of his room. You could tell from his bedroom that Edison was dinosaur mad. The wallpaper had a dinosaur pattern printed onto it. Posters and wall planners all depicted prehistoric creatures of various sorts. On his shelves he had plastic figurines of colourful dinosaurs, a stone ammonite, colourful stickers, a fossilised sharks tooth, and couple of photos from his few visits to the zoo. He had found much of his collection at car boot sales, charity shops and jumble sales. Some of the second-hand ones were a bit chewed and faded, but generally good enough for him.

He covered the whole wall opposite his bed with his own drawings and paintings of prehistoric creatures, and on his bedroom door was a large sign featuring a roaring Tyrannosaurus Rex with the words 'Keep out - or Die!' in a speech bubble coming out of its bloody mouth.

His most embarrassing dinosaur was a soft cuddly toy that sat on his bed. This was an old furry Brontosaurus that his Mum had bought him, but that he now felt too old for.

"It's got a hot water bottle hidden inside it." said his Mum. "Clever isn't it?"

"Yes Mum," Edison replied. "It's really nice."

He kept it, as he didn't want to upset her.

In his room he would often plan out his own miniature dinosaur zoo on the bedroom floor using his assortment of plastic figurines, blocks of Lego, model buildings taken from an old train set, empty food containers, yogurt pots etc. This was his private zoo. Here he could happily play for hours, either on his own, or with Orla, although she wasn't that interested in these games nowadays. He remembered that even his Mum would sometimes play the dinosaur game with him, but that was before Alex came along.

Edison knew most of the prehistoric creature's names and one of his larger posters charted different dinosaur periods and where their fossils had been discovered in the world. Edison dreamed of visiting these places one day. So far he had only left England once and that was to travel to Scotland to visit Granny Nell and Granddad Roy before they moved to Spain. Mandy didn't have the money to take them on foreign holidays and Alex would never want to anyway. He hated foreigners and their food, "foreign muck", was what he called it. Strange, as he loved an Indian take-away at the weekend.

Mum still occasionally came into his bedroom to tidy up and Edison always knew that she had been there as the stuffed Brontosaurus hot water bottle would be left posed in humorous positions. Edison would find it reading a book, snuggled up under the duvet, or even sticking its head out, as if hiding, from the laundry basket. Edison didn't mind as this often put a smile on his face.

Edison could often smell the zoo from his bedroom window, depending on which way the wind was blowing. Dinosaurs fart all the time! They just can't stop burping and breaking wind. Fossilised farts mixed with Prehistoric 'Parps', leaving the air heavy with the scent of all manner of partly digested food.

He lived on the first floor in the only block of housing association flats in this part of Clifthill. Sadly he didn't have a view of the zoo, but at night he would lean out of his window to hear the sounds of the creatures, their prehistoric grunts and farts exploding into the night sky like a scented firework display.

The neighbours in their big houses didn't mind the grunts and roars of the dinosaurs at all hours, sometimes in the middle of the night - but they did mind the smell. The locals had nicknamed the 'Fart Park'. The scent of rotten cabbage didn't go down well when you are trying to hold a fantastic garden party, a charity fundraiser or a the cafe was the best alternative. Hence the over inflated prices for its tea, coffee and cakes!

Edison would push to the front of the crowd and gaze down from the huge windows in wonder at the interior of zoo. On quieter days he could spend hours there watching and drawing in his notebooks. He was a pretty good artist.

Edison picked up the letter. The zoos metallic logo shimmered brilliantly in the light. The design was a blue silhouette of a Tyrannosaurus Rex within a circular capital letter D. Below the logo was the message, 'Greetings from the only Dinosaur zoo in the world'. The envelope felt heavy as if it had several sheets of paper inside. Surely this was a good thing wasn't it? Edison thought. Rejection letters were usually light, weren't they?

He held it, his hands shaking, nervous about opening it. What if it was just another rejection? He already knew that he was probably too young to work at the zoo, even part time at weekends. Although he would be thirteen in only a week's time, he still imagined that the zoo would think him too young.

So far he had written 101 application letters, over a period of nearly two years, with few replies. There had been just three standard rejection letters. All said much the same - "Thank you but, *blah blah*, no vacancies, blah blah, lots of other excellent candidates, blah, we will of course keep your letter in our records."

"You're wasting your time." Alex told him as he whittled away at yet another of his monstrous wood carvings. Alex liked to make wooden Totem poles in the flats communal garden; no one was sure why, but it really annoyed the neighbours. Alex was no craftsman and his carvings were horrendous and ugly. Residents had petitioned the housing association to take action to remove them, but so far nothing had happened. They stood littering the garden, solid and sentinel, causing the residents grief.

It was Edison's ambition to work at the zoo. Since his first visit two years ago he had been writing to the zoo most weeks applying for a part time weekend job. These positions were few and very hard to come by. No one at Edison's school worked there. He had never met anyone else that had. Once he had seen a boy interviewed on the local news who worked Saturdays and school holidays at the zoo. He had been talking about chopping up the vegetables for food and cleaning out the dinosaur pens. The boy seemed very well-to-do. He said he particularly liked the Triceratops and had named each one individually. Edison wasn't sure why the news crew had chosen to interview him, but guessed it wasn't for his charisma.

As he was under 16, and a local resident, he could have had a season ticket, at a reduced rate. However Alex, had said that it was a 'rip off' and far too expensive, and that he wasn't going to pay for it. So Edison had only been inside the zoo twice, once on a school trip, and another time with his grandparents. The zoo trip had been a special occasion, when they had last visited, two years ago. He treasured the zoo guide book with its fold-out map that they had bought for him. The map hung, in pride of place, on his bedroom wall, surrounded by other Dinosaur memorabilia. He knew the map by heart and believed he would be able to walk

He was now the European Chairman of Huge Food Incorporated and as such the second most important member of the organisation. The only person superior to him was the American chairman, the secretive Stephen Black. Jacobi and Stephen didn't always see eye to eye and there was much competition between them. Stephen was an ex bodybuilder who had let his once hued frame go a little to seed. He favoured a blond crew cut and Hawaiian shirts whereas Jacobi always wore a pale grey suit and had immaculately groomed dark hair. If a passerby came across them together they might well be mistaken for an elderly surfer with his friend from the funeral directors. Stephen insisted on informally calling Jacobi 'Jac', which he found patronising and annoying.

"Jac, you gotta come over more and visit us," said Stephen earlier that day on the phone. "We miss you, Buddy".

Jacobi doubted very much that Stephen Black missed him at all, and that the offer was just another ploy to drag Jacobi away from Huge Foods UK London headquarters. Last time he had visited the United States Jacobi had returned to find US staff, appointed by Stephen, had 'by coincidence', visited the London offices whilst he was away. By all accounts they had been rude, upset staff and demanded to see all of the Huge Foods UK research materials. What they had been digging for wasn't apparent, but Jacobi had decided not to visit the US headquarters for quite a while.

"I miss you too Stephen," Jacobi lied. "But we are far too busy here at the moment".

Jacobi needed a brilliant new idea. A range of foods that would appeal to every child and pestered parent in the country. Products that would propel Huge Food Inc to the top of the tree. Jacobi didn't intend on retiring until he had created something new and amazing, to wipe that smug smile off Stephen Blacks pudgy face.

He had been sitting quietly for nearly an hour and he knew that his alarm clock would soon go off. Ideas had been popping into his mind, but not necessarily good ones. He immediately stored these away in deep sections of his brain labelled 'maybe for later', 'dump it' or 'that is possibly the most stupid idea you have ever had'.

One concept that wouldn't go away and had actually popped up before was dinosaurs. Since the arrival of the Dinosaur zoo in Clifthill the public's appetite for all things dinosaur was vast.

Stick a picture of a dinosaur on the foods packaging and they would fly off the shelves. But the timing was always crucial. One minute you could be selling thousands of dinosaur shaped chicken bits, and then hardly any. Children could be fickle and get bored easily. It often took a new film or popular book to get the market booming again.

Jacobi had read yet another newspaper article about the eccentric scientist Dr Harriet May, Director of the zoo. He hadn't really taken a lot of interest in the article at the time but now something nagged and squirreled about in his brain. He had always been frustrated that Dr May and her precious Dinosaur zoo wouldn't go into partnership with him and Huge Foods on a series of products. Huge Foods had made many offers of sponsorship, even offering Dr May a non executive position on the board at Huge Foods, but the zoo would never offer its patronage or allow its official logo to be used.

"The Dinosaur zoo, as you know Mr Magnuson, doesn't endorse food products," said the curt public relations official representing the zoo. "We only ever allow our unique branding to be used by carefully selected charities."

Dr. May herself was almost impossible to meet face to face or even talk to on the telephone. She kept herself hidden away in the zoo laboratories, only venturing out when needed to help publicise the zoo and its scientific work.

Jacobi picked up his pen, a silver Mont Blanc, and jotted something down in the small leather notebook sitting on the table in front of him. He wrote - 'Dinosaurs. Zoo. Size. Research'. He then underlined the word 'Size', snapped the notebook shut, stood up and left the room.

Chapter 04
Saturday - The First Day.

Edison ran to the zoo that first day, incredibly excited, wondering what he would be doing and who he may meet. He didn't mind if he spent all day just clearing out dinosaur dung, even if it was his birthday, at least he would be working at the zoo! The night before he had hardly slept and he still had butterflies dancing about inside his belly.

"I've put some clean clothes out for you on your bed." His Mum told Edison as he ate an early birthday breakfast of toast, cereal and birthday cake. The cake was of course in the shape of a dinosaur with a huge number thirteen iced onto it. A group of birthday cards stood on the table in front of him. He hoped for others to open this evening when he returned from the zoo, as so far there hadn't been a card from his Grandparents.

Edison had already told his Mum that he should wear old clothing for the zoo.

"I'm bound to get really muddy and dirty." He explained.

"You are not starting your first day at the zoo in dirty clothing." His Mum argued, "I don't want them thinking you're a scruff, especially on your birthday!"

stone arched doorway next to the gates that the general public would hardly give a second glance. A small sign stated "Private - Employees only. Please ring bell for attention". Edison noticed a key coded entry pad next to the sign. The bell was a brass replica profile of a Tyrannosaurus head. Edison pressed the dinosaurs eye, the bells button, and the mouth opened to reveal a speech intercom hidden behind its teeth.

"Hello?" A crackly voice came out of the dinosaur speaker.

For a moment Edison was stuck for words. Slightly panicked, he couldn't think what to say.

"Hello?" repeated the voice.

"Oh umm, Hi, my name's Edison, Edison Hope. The new Saturday boy."

"Stay there, I will come down and let you in."

Edison stood on the step next to the doors. He looked so small in comparison to the large doorway. This was the beginning of a new chapter in his life, and though he felt nervous, he also knew just how lucky he was.

A receptionist opened the door and led Edison into a large, airy, waiting area. Built of stone, with a high vaulted ceiling, it reminded Edison of some churches he had been into. Each of the solid walls had thick wooden benches recessed into them. Large photographic posters of the zoo and its dinosaurs hung behind perspex displays on the walls and a huge fossilised skeleton of a Dilophosaurus stood up-lit on a plinth at the back of the room.

"Take a seat Edison," Said the smiley receptionist. "Reg Green, our head keeper will be down in a minute. He will show you around today."

"Thank you." Edison replied.

The receptionist smiled and walked off, her footsteps echoing down the corridor.

Edison sat down on one of the wooden benches, folding his arms. The room was chilly and silent. He spent some time reading the posters but after ten minutes he was still alone. Edison noticed some old graffiti carved into the dark wood. The initials and dates had been carved carefully and intricately, nothing like modern graffiti. He ran his finger into the deep grooves of "A.N.Holmes 1845". This name must have been carved only a few years after the zoo had been first established. He wondered who A.N.Holmes had been.

He got up and went over to investigate the fossilised Dilophosaurus skeleton. It towered above him standing at least twelve feet tall. The skeleton was brilliantly exhibited, standing solid and proud, and at first it was hard for Edison to see what gave the bones their strength to stay upright like this. He then noticed the semi-hidden metal framework that acted as scaffolding holding the whole fossilised creature together. The skeleton seemed almost complete, with a few missing bones reconstructed out of a clay coloured plastic. The rooms lighting cast shadows of the bones across the ceiling and walls making it seem even larger and imposing. What really stood out was its open mouth full of sharp meat eating teeth. The skull of the Dilophosaurus had its trade mark cranial crests attached, looking like a devils horns in the dramatic lighting.

The brass plaque underneath the dinosaur stated that it had been discovered by Dr Harriet May in 1985 in South Dakota, USA. Edison had known that before establishing the Dinosaur zoo Dr. Harriet May had been studying fossils as a palaeontologist. This must have been one of her most precious finds.

"She's impressive, isn't she?"

Edison jumped and turned around. A large man of about 55 with a short trimmed greying beard, wearing zoo overalls and a black t-shirt stood before him. The t-shirt had a white 'Motorhead' logo printed onto it. The man looked healthy and strong with huge muscular arms.

"Hi Ed." He said holding out a giant hand and firmly shaking Edison's. "I see that you have met Doris."

"Doris?" said Edison, taken aback, nursing his squashed hand.

"Dead Doris, the deceased Dilophosaurus," Chuckled Reg. "One of Dr Harriet's most amazing finds."

He slapped Edison heartily on the shoulder, nearly causing him to lose his footing and topple into the fossilised Dinosaur.

"I'll show you some real, living Dilophosaurus, later on."

Edison regained his composure; he now knew who he was speaking to.

"I'm Reg Green, Head Keeper." Reg chuckled. "And today will be one of the most amazing days of your life!"

#

Reg Green had been employed at the zoo all of his working life, starting as a teenager. He had simply left school one Friday and started at the zoo on the following Monday. Life was easier in those days.

True, he had done very well at school, and always expressed an interest in animals. It may have also helped that his father was the dentist to the then zoo owner, Wilfred May. Old Mr. May had a life long fear of dentistry and perhaps Reg's fathers calm hands and caring manner had helped his son get his first job as an assistant in the reptile house.

It seemed such a long time ago. Reg was one of the few remaining staff to have seen the zoo transform from a small city animal zoo into what it is now, the only Dinosaur zoo in the world.

Reg hadn't found the changes taxing when Dr Harriet arrived to take control of the zoo. Many colleagues had left once they realised that their beloved lions or penguins were getting the push. They moved to other UK zoos, often transferring with their specialist animals.

Reg felt that they hadn't seen the amazing possibilities of developing the first zoo for dinosaurs. Reg was loyal to Dr Harriet and remembered her from her student intern days at the zoo. She had been keen and obviously intelligent. He felt embarrassed now to think that he had once managed her, and often had her clean out the many reptile vivariums, or helping to chop the huge amounts of fruit and vegetables needed to feed some of the animals. She had never complained, at least not to Reg anyway. It was obvious even then that the quiet, polite palaeontology student was destined for greater things. Her mind may have been more in the world of fossils and prehistoric creatures, than the day to day workings of the zoo, but she was an incredibly conscientious and hard worker.

It wasn't really a surprise that when Wilfred May, Harriet's uncle, passed away that he left the zoo to Harriet and her brother, Hadley, in his will. He had no other family, and his constant battles with the local authorities left him with little inclination to leave the zoo to the city council. He didn't really trust the authorities and believed that they would probably have sold the zoo to private developers. He wasn't going to see his life's work and his legacy destroyed like that. Whether he would have approved of the changes his niece had made to his precious Animal zoo, Reg wasn't sure. But he did believe that old Mr. May would have been very proud of her for creating the worlds first Dinosaur zoo.

Edison had of course read much about Reg Green in his zoo books and magazines. Reg was a bit of a legend in the animal world and his eccentric character came across as hugely charismatic on television, making Reg a big hit with the public.

Reg had been Head of the Reptiles and Amphibians before Dr Harriet had discovered her way of creating and resurrecting extinct dinosaurs. Because of his reptile experience Reg became Dr Harriet's right hand man when the zoo became exclusively a menagerie for prehistoric creatures. Though a private man, Reg was happy to help publicise the zoo, its charities and its scientific advancements when required. The zoo was his life.

"A.N Holmes was one of our illustrious founding fathers." Reg pointed to the initials carved into the wooden bench. "He was only 24 at the time he brought the land for the zoo. For the grand sum of £3,000 pounds! That was a lot of money in 1843."

Reg pointed to another name, W.T. May, inscribed in the old wood. "Walter Thomas May, he helped establish the original zoo along with Andrew Nicholas Holmes."

"Walter was Dr Harriet May's grandfather?" Edison asked.

"Great grandfather, but good lad, I can see you know your zoo history" Reg replied.

"I have some books on the zoo." Edison said.

"And many more on dinosaurs, no doubt?" Reg joked.

Edison laughed and said yes, just a few.

"Well good," Reg said. "No point working in the world's only Dinosaur zoo if you don't like ruddy dinosaurs, is there?" Reg puffed himself up, made his arms rigid, face bulge and waddled on the spot. He seemed to be doing a strange impression of one of the creatures. Edison wasn't sure *which* dinosaur, but he chuckled all the same. He had the feeling that Reg Green was a little mad.

"Well let's get the day started!" said Reg. He looked at his watch. "You turned up on time, five minutes early in fact. So that's a good start. Tick!" Reg ticked an imaginary sheet with an imaginary pencil.

On a low table in front of the lockers was a pile of new clothing. Reg reached down and passed them to Ed.

"Right, here's your official zoo overalls. Please wear them at all times inside the zoo. Otherwise you may get mistaken for Joe Public." He handed Ed two pairs of overalls.

"Next we have two official T-shirts and baseball cap." He passes these to Edison.

"Between you and me I think the T-shirts are rubbish, but feel free to wear them."

Edison held the clothing, his arms outstretched. Reg stuck the baseball cap onto Edison's head.

"Right, you go and get into those and I'll put the kettle on. See you next door in the kitchen when you're ready." Reg walked out of the locker room.

"I can't start the tour without a hot cup of char." He shouted.

Edison looked about the empty room. Nearly all of the lockers had their owners names stuck onto them. One name was familiar to him, 'Bob Soup'. It wasn't really a common surname and he felt sure that he had heard it before.

Chapter 05
The Missing Finger.

Edison returned to the staff canteen now fully attired in pristine zoo overalls and wearing his baseball cap.

"Very smart," Reg said. "You really look the part."

"Thanks!" Edison said, adjusting his cap.

Reg was leaning against one of the kitchen units drinking from a huge mug of tea.

Edison started to look around the room and was amazed to see a group of his letters and drawings pinned up on the huge notice board. The same wall was covered with photographs of the zoo, the dinosaurs, its keepers and staff. Thank-you letters from school parties who had enjoyed their visits were pinned up onto the board. There was also a selection of photographs of celebrities and world leaders who had visited over the years. A signed picture of Reg and Dr May shaking hands with the last President of the USA took pride of place. In it the group stood in front of a large pterodactyl, which was hanging upside down from a branch. Edison was immediately reminded of the close encounter he had with one of these creatures just last week. The

"But I have a large map of the zoo hanging on my wall."

"Excellent," Reg replied, "So you'll know your way around the public areas. Eventually you will be shown all of our secret routes around the zoo too."

"Secret?" Edison asked.

"We have a network of private paths and hidden entrances to the enclosures." Reg explained. "It helps speed things up and keeps us out of the way of the public."

Edison had guessed that to feed the dinosaurs, clean out the enclosures, and even to move the creatures around that there must be a system like this. It allowed the keepers unrestricted access to the dinosaurs, to do their work, away from curious members of the public, for safety reasons if nothing else.

"Let's start with the Stegs." Reg said, leading the way to a large enclosure surrounded by mature trees and foliage. "We have tried to give them a varied enclosure. The trees provide shelter, but the bark also gives them something to scratch themselves against."

As if on cue a Stegosaurus, about the size of an adult rhinoceros, started to rub its rump against a large tree trunk.

"As you can see." Reg said.

The Stegosaurus let out what seemed to be satisfied grunt.

"Got an itchy arse Harold?" Reg Shouted.

Edison giggled.

“The bushes give them a place to hide, when the public’s interest gets too much for them."

Edison could see that the enclosure was double fenced. A narrow moat had been dug in front of the fences to keep the public at a safe distance. The zoo didn't want the possibility of someone putting their arm through the fence and getting it bitten off. Occasional accidents like this had happened in other zoos where lions had made a tasty meal of the arms of stupid visitors who had tried to stroke and ‘pet’ the hungry cats.

"The inner fence is electrified," Reg remarked. "So be careful when ever you’re cleaning the enclosures. Make sure that the current has been switched off. It won't kill you, but it will give you an awful poke!"

Reg looked down at Edison.

"A lad like you will get blown off his feet."

"Where are all the others?" Edison asked, looking at the single bum scratching Stegosaurus in the enclosure.

"Oh they are probably still inside." Reg replied. "Let's go have a look."

Reg and Edison went down a side path that led into a darker underground passage with glass viewing windows. On the other side of the thick glass was a large room, its floor covered in dense leaves, straw and foliage. Edison could see the hulking shapes of various Stegosaurus as they lay slumped on the floor, some looked to be sleeping. The unlit room smelt strongly of dinosaur manure and urine.

"As you know, none of our mature dinosaurs have ever grown to anything bigger than an elephant or rhinoceros.” Reg remarked. "Dr Harriet's method for resurrecting the dinosaurs still has many flaws."

considered lucky to get splashed by these, 'Pterodactyl trophies', but most visitors hoped not to be that fortunate!

"The Pterodactyls are pretty laid back, but the wire helps to stop any accidents." Reg remarked. "We don't want any kiddie's inquisitive fingers getting bitten off, do we?"

One of the creatures flew down from the rocky outcrop onto the mesh screen in front of them, making Edison jump. The creature let out deep squawks similar to that of a raven. Edison was close enough to smell its fishy breath.

"Hello Ted!" Reg smiled at the Pterodactyl. The creature squawked back.

"Ted?" Edison asked, trying not to breathe.

"Ted is our tamest. We use him for the displays and sticking on the shoulders of visiting celebs."

Edison realised that Ted was the Pterodactyl that he had come face to face with just last week. Excitedly he nearly told Reg this, but stopped himself. He wasn't sure what Reg would think of him climbing the tree to look down on the zoo.

"Ted has been a little naughty lately," Reg said, "Causing all sorts of mischief."

"Really?" Edison remarked. He didn't ask Reg to elaborate. He knew very well one of the things Ted had done.

The Pterodactyl climbed down off the mesh using its long claws and hopped onto the ground. It then walked away towards the edge of the water pool and plunged in. Edison could see it under the water, gliding effortlessly, as if flying. It surfaced with a plump wriggling fish in its mouth. The Pterodactyl tossed its head back, opened its beak, and like a pelican, swallowed the fish down in one slippery gulp.

A sign on the wall stated:

'Danger - Don't feed the Pterodactyls - They Bite!'

"Have there ever been any accidents?" asked Edison looking at the sign.

Reg looked thoughtful.

"One silly schoolboy lost a finger once, in the early days."

"What happened?"

"They sewed it back on at the hospital." Reg replied.

Edison looked worried.

"Well in actual fact they couldn't find the original finger, as the Pterodactyl had gone and swallowed it. So they amputated one of his toes, a big toe, and sewed that on in its place." Reg explained.

Edison felt a little queasy. Having a big toe cut off to surgically make a 'Toe Finger' didn't sound good.

"He works here now; he's one of the keepers, Bob Soup." Reg said. "He will show you the scar, if you ask him."

Bob soup. The name he had seen written on one of the lockers in the staff room. Who was this fingerless Bob Soup? Edison knew the name; he must have read about the accident before, in one of his zoo books.

As they left the enclosure Edison noticed a colour poster on the wall. It showed an injured hand, missing a finger, the wound all bloody and torn. Next to the photo was an illustration of a Pterodactyl with the words 'Yum Yum', in a cartoon speech bubble, coming out of its beak.

"It reminds the public not to do anything stupid." Reg said.

Edison felt a little ill. He didn't think that he would be asking Bob Soup, the toe fingered keeper, for a look at his reconstructed hand any time soon.

#

Dominic sat on a low stone wall drinking from a can of Cola and skiving work. He really hated cleaning dinosaur enclosures out, their cages always stank. All he ever seemed to be doing was moving wet piles of muck from one stinking place to another. He skulked behind some bushes, hoping not to be seen, but able to hear if anyone started coming down the path. Dominic squashed the can and tossed it over his head and into the bushes. Someone else could clean that up later, he decided.

Dominic White was fifteen, tall and passed for older, having no difficulty in getting served in pubs. His lanky frame was unattractive, mostly because he had developed a creepy stoop. He had thick black gelled hair, swished into a boy band style. He really didn't look like he should be working in a zoo. He had never wanted to work there in the first place. His parents had persuaded him that it would be good for the family if he got a job at the zoo. His Dad had pulled some strings, and voila, he had a weekend job. After a few weeks his Dad asked him to keep an ear out for any sort of useful information.

"Like what?" Dominic asked.

"I'm interested in finding out how Dr. May has managed to bring the dinosaurs back from extinction." His Dad replied.

"Yeah, good luck with that!" Dominic sarcastically replied. "You and the rest of the world want that information."

At first Dominic wasn't sure that his old man was serious, but it soon became apparent that he really was interested in the zoos secrets.

"I won't be able to get anywhere near the labs," Dominic explained. "Or Dr Harriet's office."

"Just keep an eye out for anything interesting," His Dad told him. "Any notes or files lying about. Any gossip you may hear."

His Dad was secretive about his work but Dominic understood it to be something in the money markets. After a year of toiling at the ruddy zoo Dominic hadn't found anything of substance to tell him. All he could concretely tell his Dad was that dinosaurs shat a lot, and it stank. His Dad told him to 'just keep at it.'

Dominic's family was wealthy and lived in a large townhouse only a few streets away from the zoo. Dominic was a day pupil at the local private school, Clifthill College. It was the same expensive school that Dr Harriet had attended as a child. It may have been that connection that had helped his Dad get him the weekend job. Clifthill College dated back to 1852 and so was nearly as old as the original zoo itself.

Footsteps approached the enclosure and Dominic heard voices. It sounded like that oaf Reg Green. Dominic quickly jumped up, grabbed his broom, and started to furiously sweep the path.

"Ah, Dominic." Reg said as he rounded the corner.

Dominic looked up and stopped pretending to sweep.

"Hi Mr. Green." He waved to Reg and then saw the small boy standing next to him, kitted out in a pristine zoo uniform. The boy looked a couple of years younger than himself and a bit wimpy.

"This is Edison, our new weekend boy." Reg said.

"Hi." Edison smiled.

"Dominic is another part-timer like you." Reg told Edison. "He started here a year ago."

The two lads shook hands awkwardly and Edison automatically felt uneasy with the older boy. There was something about him that seemed untrustworthy. Dominic took little interest in Edison and thought, if anything, that he looked a bit poor.

"I'm giving Edison the guided tour, later on I'll bring him back, and you can show him the ropes." Reg said.

"OK Mr Green," Dominic replied. "He can help me clean out the Segisaurus."

"Maybe not the 'Sid's', Dominic." Reg said. "Those are a little too nasty for a first day!"

The Segisaurus where nicknamed the 'Sid's' at the zoo due to their uncanny resemblance to the dead punk singer, Sid Vicious. They where skinny, wild and actually pretty vicious. Like the singer they where often covered in bloody cuts caused by fighting with each other. The 'Sid's' also had a crest of spiky blue and orange fur sprouting out of the tops of their heads, similar to a punk rockers Mohican haircut.

Reg turned and guided Edison away down the path. Edison looked back and was sure he caught a glimpse of Dominic giving them a rude hand gesture, but he couldn't be sure, as he was now giving a jolly wave.

"See you *lay-terrr!*" Dominic sang mischievously.

Strange lad, thought Edison, very odd.

ground gases had been made over millions of years from the decomposing bodies of animals and vegetation. Could it be possible that dinosaurs had left their markers in the gas as they had left their bones preserved in rock? Would there be the equivalent of a gaseous 'DNA'? Could she then detect, collect and unravel the secrets of these gases?

Could she date them, as you could age a tree from counting its rings? Was there a way to isolate the vapours and develop a new identification technique and use this to recreate or replicate the dinosaurs?

It seemed an idiotic idea, but the identification and extraction of DNA from blood, tissue and bone, had only been a relatively recent discovery. Many years ago this also would have seemed improbable, impossible even. The scientists Crick and Watson had made their scientific breakthroughs in the 1950's, fifty years later the whole human genome was mapped out.

She remembered reading about the regions American Indian tribes, such as the Dakota and Cheyenne, and how their rituals often involved shape shifting and out of body experiences. Dancing and chanting, with the aid of mysterious potions, propelling them into other realms. Could they too have been under the influence of these invisible gases?

Harriet couldn't get the vision of seeing herself walking amongst living dinosaurs out of her mind. It seemed a premonition of things to come.

On later expeditions she developed an unusual method for collecting the gas, which was safe, but eccentric. She used special self-inflating balloons, which only enlarged when oxygen levels decreased. The balloons would be laid flat, like little rubber fish, on the soil. If gas was present they would twitch and wiggle and slowly inflate, sucking in the vapours emitted from deep beneath the earth. Harriet could leave the balloons, tethered across a wide area, coming back to collect them if and when they inflated, like a gamekeeper setting traps. She could easily carry hundreds of them empty in their flat inert state. When inflated the landscape became full of multicoloured balloons, colours vivid against the dusty brown soil, gently swaying in the wind like strange desert flowers. Harriet walked back buoyantly to her field base like an eccentric balloon seller, covered in the gas filled balloons.

When she inherited the zoo Harriet had immediately set about building and developing the specialist Egg Lab and had purchased some of the best scientific machinery she could find. She sourced sensitive analysis machines from the petrochemical, forensic and perfume industries. These units analysed gas and chemicals and broke them down into their constituent parts. The computers analysed patterns that emerged, or detected unique pointers in the vapours. These would be collected and synthetically amplified. The smells that occasionally emitted from The Egg Lab in its early days where so fowl that many residents living nearby complained. The council and health authority insisted that the zoo install state of the art air filtering systems to take away the whiff.

Hadley, Harriet's brother, who had co-inherited the zoo along with her from their Uncle was dubious, at first. He saw huge profits leaving the zoo, going towards the new laboratory, instead of going into his pockets.

This was Alex's domain. Edison refused to even get in the car and that was fine with Alex. He didn't need, or want, to ferry kids about. Once a week he dropped Mandy off at their local Asda to do the weeks shop. He would remain sitting in the car, listening to loud music, and ogling up strangers. He was proud of his car and wanted everyone to know it, always hoping that one of the passing 'yummy mummy's' would be impressed by his wheels. They just blanked him and muttered 'idiot' under their breaths.

Alex couldn't be bothered going into the store. Anyway he was known to the supermarkets security for nicking stuff in the past. He was probably still on their ban list. Once Mandy had filled the cars boot with the weeks shopping, and got in, he would screech out of the car park, music blaring. If she moaned he would tell her, 'to take a bleeding taxi next time, if you don't like it'.

Twice a week Alex treated himself to a cooked breakfast at The Spoon. He didn't rate Mandy's breakfasts at all.

"She can't cook a bleeding fried egg, let alone the full works!" He was often heard to say to Mr. D.

The Spoon was a small dirty cafe that only really catered for locals and the occasional lost tourist, passing on their way to look for the zoo. The cafes 'Full English' came with a twist; a free, complimentary can of 'Hawk', a cheap, but strong, lager. For the cider drinkers, such as Alex, a can of 'Blade', an even stronger brew.

Here Alex could meet his mates and have a bit of a morning pick me up as well. All of Alex's mates chose The Spoons 'Full English'. The sausages may have been a bit tough, the bacon chewy, and the tea thick like mud, but the 'Hawk' and 'Blade' made it slip down easily. They would all sit, squeezed together, on greasy plastic seats, at sticky sauce stained tables, spending the morning joking and winding each other up. Easy banter, with just a hint of menace, drifted around the small sweaty room. A fried food fog fell as oily condensation, dripping down the glass windows. This thick, heavy atmosphere, made it hard for anyone outside the cafe to see inside, and even harder to enter. It was a brave stranger who chose to wander in unexpectedly.

The Spoon was one of the cities key meeting places for a selection of it's less salubrious residents. It was home-from-home for a rough ragbag of burglars, gamblers, druggies, scumbags, layabouts and petty criminals. You wouldn't find many 'Mister Bigs' eating there, not unless you counted Mr. Douglas, and he owned the gaff. If you wanted to buy a cheap DVD player, car stereo or other knock off items, at knock down prices, The Spoon was the place to be. It was well known to the police, who knew, that like bees to a hive, the local criminals congregated there. When they wanted to pick up a suspect, all they needed to do was park up around the corner, and discreetly pull the criminal in as they passed by, on their way to The Spoon.

Alex's nick name in the cafe was 'Wurzel', due to his love of cider and terrible taste in music. When drunk he would serenade everyone with his rendition of the song 'I am a cider drinker' by The Wurzels.

Alex's drinking and criminal activities often forced Mandy to kick him out of the flat. He would reappear, a few nights later, banging on the flats locked door and windows in the early hours of the morning.

“Mandy, love, let me in.” Alex would plead through the letterbox.

Tap, tap, tap, on the window.

“Pleeeeassse.” He would slur, trying to see inside the bedroom window, “I love you *darling*.”

Usually he would start trying to get back into Mandy’s good books by sounding sensitive and remorseful, but this escalated to banging and shouting, as he eventually got more frustrated. His angry banging would then start to wake the rest of the flats residents.

One night Alex had tried to climb into the flat via an open window, by standing on a black wheelie rubbish bin. Mandy had locked him out and was lying in bed, purposely ignoring his cries. Alex lost his balance, his feet slipping on the smooth plastic lid, and the bin shot out from under him. He toppled drunkenly into the neighbours’ garden, the contents of the bin landing around him as he fell into their flowerbed. He lay sprawled in the foliage, bits of smelly rubbish spread over him. A neighbour later told Mandy that she had seen Alex trying to crawl into the overturned bin and go to sleep. Needless to say, the neighbours liked Alex about as much as Edison did.

On nights like these Edison would stay in his bed, groggy eyed, and listen to the events unfolding outside. Inevitably his Mum would relent and give in, just for the sake of the neighbours getting some sleep, and allow him back into the flat. Edison would hear Alex’s whining apologies as his Mum made coffee and toast to help sober him up. Why his Mum put up with Alex he wasn’t sure. As far as Edison could see the man had few redeeming features and was more of a hindrance, than a help. Edison really couldn't believe that his Mum was 'in love' with Alex. If this was her taste in men, then what must his biological father have been like?

"I wish I had a Dad like yours." Edison would tell Orla.

"Dad's great," Orla replied. "But I really only see him at weekends."

"I wish it was the same with Alex." Edison replied. "I'm at the zoo weekends, so I wouldn't have to see him at all!"

Chapter 08
The Weird and the Wild.

Bob Soup sat, hidden away, in one of the more private gardeners sheds reading 'The Weird and the Wild', a monthly animal magazine he subscribed too. This publication dealt in stories about animal accidents both in captivity and the wild. Seeing others terrible accidents and injuries lightened his humour a little. It was sad to bask in others misfortunes, he knew, but he would be lying if he said it didn't make him feel a bit better about himself.

True he had been the stupid one to put his finger through the wire mesh barrier in the first place. If one of his mates hadn't dared him too, he would still have his original finger now. He couldn't honestly say that the accident had left him 'mentally' scarred, but he did hate his replacement finger, almost as much as he hated those pterodactyls!

Zoos across the world had accidents involving their animals, staff and the visiting public. Bob Soup knew this, but it didn't help him feel any better about losing his own finger in a zoo 'incident'. Most of his life he had put up with taunts and jibes about his ugly 'toe finger'. He was of course happy that the thing functioned as it should, he could grip and hold anything that he needed to, the graft was effective, but why hadn't they made it look a bit more pretty?

He flicked through the colourfully vivid magazine stopping on a story about a large cat attack at a German zoo. A naked drunk had climbed into the lion enclosure and died. The article featured tourist snaps of the whole incident. An overweight, pot bellied, and unusually hairy man climbed over the spiked iron railings, dangerous enough in itself when you are nude, and jumped down into the enclosure. The lions treated the large man as a toy, a plaything perhaps, a fat hairy ball. But their sharp claws still ripped him to shreds, burst him, before the rescuers arrived. It was said that the victim might have done it because he was depressed. Bob wasn't surprised; just look at him, too many beers and bratwurst sausages that one. Strangely the victim had kept his traditional green alpine hat on during the whole sorry ordeal.

Bob had heard of keepers getting over confident with their animals, too casual, and letting their guard down. Nonchalantly going about their tasks. Forgetting that the carnivorous captive tiger or lion was crouched behind them, about to pounce. Keepers getting maimed or killed by their charges happened more often than most people expected. Seemingly tame and domesticated creatures could turn back into their wild, natural state in a flash.

Bears had been know to strike out at the public, if folks strayed too close to the cage bars. A furry paw would flash out like lightning, and snare the passing visitor, pulling them in. Visitor's arms and legs got bitten off long before help arrived. A zoo could post as many warning signs as it liked, but stupid people would still act idiotically, that was life.

gates and getting their heads bitten off faded. The locals took the zoo to their hearts and it had become the unofficial mascot of the city.

Then the adolescent Bob Soup went and got his finger bitten off!

Everything went haywire for a while.

As head keeper Reg Green had tried to retrieve the lost finger from the pterodactyl enclosure. Sadly it had already been eaten by one of the creatures. Bob would always be indebted to Reg for at least trying. After the accident Reg visited him convalescing at home, and it was at that moment Bob had decided to try and become a zoo keeper.

Bob put down the magazine and looked at his watch. He had been killing time until the lunch hour and now seemed like a good time to head over to the canteen. Even though he was a thin, pale man, he often felt hungry and had a surprisingly large appetite.

His mobile phone buzzed and Bob looked at the text message. Recently he had been contacted by an outsider to supply some information about the zoo. It wasn't anything too confidential, just how the zoo ran day to day, that kind of thing. Bob guessed that a rival enterprise was looking to employ similar methods. He didn't feel that bad about supplying this information and the extra money would certainly help.

As he stood up he saw two lads pass by outside the sheds cobwebbed window. It was Dominic White and that new lad. No doubt he was showing the new boy around? Dominic as usual strode about, marching in front, as if he owned the place. That boy was odd, most people thought so.

Bob managed one last look at the new boy as he followed on quickly after Dom. The lad looked familiar, as if Bob had seen his face somewhere before. He wasn't sure where.

Bob rolled up the magazine and slipped it into his back pocket. He would read the rest of the fascinating stories later after lunch.

Chapter 09
The Tower.

"Come on Eddie," Dominic shouted. "Don't be a coward!"

Edison and Dominic had been cleaning out the Triceratops sleeping quarters. It was Sunday and Edison's second day at the zoo. Dominic sat on the wall, supervising, as Edison did most of the hard work. Mounds of smelly straw and dung had to be swept out of the pens and into huge piles outside, ready for composting. Dominic spent most of the time texting on his mobile phone whilst Edison worked.

It was a repeat of yesterday when Reg had left him under the supervision of Dominic, who had overseen Edison do all of the work. By the time they reached the canteen for lunch he was filthy and tired.

Edison had gotten home the evening before tired, but happy. His Mum had invited Orla over for his Birthday tea. They ate the remainder of the dinosaur shaped cake Mandy had made and drank fiery ginger beer. Edison told them all about the zoo, the Egg Lab and meeting Reg Green.

He opened his presents with them and loved the dinosaur pyjamas his Mum had brought him. She had also given him some other, less exciting clothing, such as new T-shirts and underwear. He tried to keep the underwear hidden from Orla, but she found them and fell to the floor laughing.

"Nice white pants Eddie!" She screeched in hysterics.

He felt his face starting to flush and get hotter.

Orla had however redeemed herself by getting him an expensive looking sketchpad with a blue metal cover which had dinosaur silhouette's embossed into it.

"I knew you'd love it!" She exclaimed excitedly.

Edison balanced his broom against the wall and wiped the sweat off his forehead.

"It's not lunchtime yet." Dominic said, looking at his watch.

It was approaching midday and Edison was really looking forward to getting something to eat and a cold drink.

"I'm thirsty." Edison replied, drinking from a bottle of water.

"How about we take a break?" Dominic suggested. "I can show you one of the zoo's secret places, if you want?"

"What about lunch?" Edison asked.

"No worries, it's on the way to the canteen anyway!" Dominic replied.

Edison felt a little dubious, and didn't really trust the older boy, but felt he had to go along with him to the canteen anyway. He was also feeling really tired from all the cleaning up. They left the huge pile of Dinosaur dung for later and shut the dens doors. The Triceratops were busy sunning themselves on the grass outside, within the electrified fence.

Dominic led Edison around the back of enclosures and behind various buildings, along a secret network of narrow pathways. These were off limits to the general public, allowing the keepers to move around the zoo without bumping into hoards of visitors all the time. Dinosaurs could also be moved safely around the park, from enclosure to enclosure, via the network of paths. Foods, bedding materials and dung ready for composting, were often all transported freely along these hidden conduits.

Edison felt lost as he steadily followed behind Dominic, who skirted quickly around the zoo. Eventually they came to a clearing and Edison recognised where they were. They stood at the foot of the deserted 'Walters Tower'. Its stone turret loomed in front of them, the wooden door bolted and locked. Edison had always wanted to go up inside the tower, but he wasn't sure that now, in the company of Dominic, was a good idea. Walters Tower was an old folly, and though it had been restored over the years, for safety reasons it was only open a few times a year to the public.

"I know a way in, around the back." Dominic smiled, as he disappeared behind the tower.

Edison knew it was a bad idea, but maybe he thought, what was wrong with just having a quick look inside?

There was a small arched window at the side of the tower; about five feet off the ground. The small stone window had no glass in it and looked just big enough for them to squeeze through. Edison watched as Dominic pulled himself up and clambered in.

"Come on Eddie." Dominic shouted, leaning out the window. "It's easy." He stuck out an arm and offered Edison a helping hand.

Edison jumped and grabbed hold of the window ledge as Dominic helped pull him through the arch and into the tower. It was very dark inside and the stone walls smelt damp and mouldy. The only light came from the small window. Edison could only just see Dominic's face, even though he was sitting right next to him on the cold stone stairs.

"Hang on." Dominic said as he fidgeted about in his pockets, and brought out a cheap plastic lighter. The interior of the tower suddenly lit up as he flicked it on. Edison could now see the dark stone walls and the spiral stone staircase climbing up above them inside the tower. Thankfully there was a wooden handrail that curved upwards against the wall. At least there would be something to hold on to as they climbed up the towers slippery steps.

"Let's go up to the top!" Dominic shouted excitedly.

He started to move quickly up the stairs leaving Edison behind in the dark. Edison followed carefully behind, his hand never leaving the ominously wobbly handrail. He soon lost sight of Dominic's lighter. As he climbed higher dusty cobwebs brushed against his face.

"Dominic!" Edison shouted down the dark staircase. "I won't be able to get down."

Dominic didn't reply, all Edison could hear were footsteps, somewhere inside of the tower.

Edison would have to go down the tower, alone, and in the pitch black. Going down the slippery steps would be even harder in the dark than going up had been.

Tentatively he stepped through the arched doorway and grabbed hold of the wooden handrail, it rattled against the wall. Slowly he started his descent. It was deadly quiet, all he could hear was his own footsteps, wet and gritty on the damp steps.

As he went further down the staircase it got darker and darker, until he was enveloped in a cold blackness. He couldn't see anything as he grabbed onto the handrail with both hands, his feet occasionally slipping on the wet stone. Although he knew that he was up high in a tower it felt like he was walking down into an underground mine or well.

He heard a noise somewhere below him and really hoped Dominic wasn't hiding, cruelly waiting patiently, ready to jump out at any moment to scare him. Edison carefully continued on down, hoping he would get to the foot of the tower soon. The small arched window that he and Dominic had entered earlier was nowhere to be seen. He wouldn't be surprised if Dominic had somehow covered it up from the outside.

The ground beneath his feet became different, more gravelly. He must have reached the bottom of the tower. Using his feet as guides he scuffed around the ground to make sure that there wasn't anymore steps. There didn't seem to be, he must be at the base of the tower. Tentatively he let go of the handrail and reached out blindly in the dark. He could just see a faint rim of light in front of his eyes. His outstretched hands touched the cold wood of the tower door. He found the handle and tried it. It turned stiffly, but the door was locked shut.

Edison wasn't sure what to do. He could bang on the door and shout for help, but would anyone even hear him? And if they did, well he wasn't even supposed to be inside the tower. It was his second day at the zoo, and already he might lose his job, if he was discovered here. It was probably best to find the window that he came through earlier, and leave the tower quietly that way, without anyone ever knowing that he had been here. He cursed Dominic for leaving him like this and started to run his hands along the cold wall, trying to find the small window.

Eventually he found the stone rim of the opening and as he had suspected Dominic had blocked it by leaning something against it from the other side. Edison pushed against the obstruction and slivers of light entered into the interior of the tower. He pushed as hard as he could but it wasn't going to be easy. The obstruction moved only inches. It felt like a large heavy board was pressed against the side of the tower. If he could manoeuvre himself into the right position he might be able to use his legs to force it out of the way.

Suddenly Edison heard a noise from outside the tower, a cough and jangle of keys. Someone was on the other side of the door and opening the rusty lock. Edison panicked, he didn't want to get into trouble, but also he felt relief that he would soon be rescued. There was nowhere to hide. Anyone coming into the tower and up the stairs would bump straight into him. He wouldn't be able to unblock the small window and escape through it in time. As the heavy door creaked open and daylight started to pour in, Edison thought the best thing that he could do was to come clean and make himself known.

"Hello?" Edison said with a quiver in his voice and momentarily blinded as his eyes adjusted to the bright sunlight.

A silhouetted figure stood in the open doorway.

"Who are you?" asked a female voice.

She wore a grey trouser suit and had a severe dark bobbed haircut.

Edison recognised her voice, before he could even focus on her face; it was Dr Harriet May, Director of the zoo!

Chapter 10
The Terrifying T-Rex.

Everyone was surprised to see Dr. Harriet May come into the canteen, accompanied by Edison, the new boy. She was a rare visitor at lunchtimes and usually ate in her office, when she remembered to eat at all. The two walked towards Reg Green who sat at a table with a mix of keepers and staff. Edison was worried that Dr. May was going to give him away, and say that she had just found him in Walters Tower. He really didn't want to get into Reg's bad books, not on his first day.

As they walked across the room, Edison saw Dominic sitting at another table and briefly caught his eye. Dominic looked away guiltily, staring down at an empty plate and fidgeting with his fork. Edison guessed Dominic thought that he was about to tell Reg of how he had been shut in the tower. But he wasn't going to, he didn't want to make even more of an enemy of Dominic. He would just be careful to stay away from him in the future.

On their walk across the zoo grounds towards the canteen, Dr. May had told Edison all about the tower, it's history, and why she liked it. She went there when she needed some 'quiet time'. Here she could get away from it all and think. She would look down on the zoo and its dinosaurs, and still feel wonder at its creation. Before leaving the tower she would always look up to the sky and thank her Uncle Wilfred for bequeathing the zoo to her.

The zoo was now so popular and financially secure that she didn't have to worry about any meddling, internal or external. Outside influences could be kept at bay and the zoo free to work on its own developments and techniques in the research labs.

The fact that her scientific methods didn't always produce dinosaurs of the correct scale troubled her. She knew that it was an amazing feat to have even resurrected the prehistoric creatures and brought them back to the world of the living. But she still felt something was amiss with her research. Most of the visiting public were thrilled to see the dinosaurs and few worried about their size. The zoo had cleverly constructed fibreglass sculptures of various types of dinosaur, to illustrate what their original, and sometimes vast, scale would have been. These models were dotted around the zoo and could be climbed up, sat on, and slid down, great fun for children and adults alike. They made for excellent publicity and photo opportunities.

"I slept in the back of my office in those days." She laughed as she told Edison, who knew much of the zoo history, but hearing it from the Dinosaur zoos creator was something he never expected. It was better than reading it in books.

"The first time we successfully hatched a living dinosaur was amazing." She explained. "I was woken in the lab at 3.30am in the morning."

Dr. Harriet had been awoken that night, to the sound of high pitch squeaks and yelping coming from the laboratory. She presumed another batch of tiny crocodiles was hatching. Their plaintive little voices pleased her. She knew that they were calling out for their mother, who would be sleeping, many meters away, in the crocodile pool. The 'mother' of these little hatch-lings, in this instance, was the "Avery 120" perspex incubator. These tanks were the safest and most reliable method for hatching reptile eggs. Under a warm thermostatically controlled heat lamp, on a bed of soft mineral vermiculite, the eggs had an excellent chance of developing. A mist of purified water, sprayed at regular intervals, kept the atmosphere moist and humid. Being born in a lab may have been sterile and unnatural, but at least it was safe and reliable. The little creatures would be well cared for when they emerged.

Dr Harriet looked at her watch, it was so early, and she groaned and sat up in the camp bed.

"I'd only been asleep for three hours." She told Edison.

The plaintive yelps coaxed her out of the relatively comfortable bed. She would go and check on the little creatures and then go back to sleep. She switched on the kettle in the labs small kitchen, the yelping masked by the boiling water. The lighting left on in the lab at night was minimal, but enough to move about in. She made herself a milky tea and yawned.

The main row of incubators was covered by a thin white cotton sheet at night. She gently lifted the corner and peered inside. None of the crocodile eggs were hatching; all of the leathery egg skins seemed clean and intact. She uncovered more of the incubators to get a closer look but the little reptilian yelps were coming from elsewhere.

A quiver of excitement stirred in Dr Harriet's stomach as she travelled along the rows of silent incubators, pulling off the white covers as she moved towards two specially adapted perspex tanks filled with the laboratories special gases. Each of these contained a solo emu egg. She hesitated and then lifted the sheet. What she saw inside made her jump and drop the mug of tea.

"Was it a dinosaur?" Edison asked in excitement.

"Not one, but two!" Dr Harriet replied.

Each of the emu eggs, in the two specialised tanks, had successfully hatched, and two baby creatures yelped for attention inside. The hatch-lings didn't look unlike infant crocodiles, but Dr Harriet knew, that at long last, she had successfully created a prehistoric dinosaur!

With the first successfully hatched baby dinosaurs came the problem of how to nurture them. Because Reg was keeper of the reptile house he was thought most experienced to organise the hand rearing. They experimented with feeding the creatures live insects, earthworms and small baby mice. Sometimes they would directly feed the creatures, a pulped meat and vegetable mush, via pipettes into their open mouths. Regrettably one of the hatched dinosaurs died within the first week, but with experience, and over time, they managed to establish a good survival rate.

Edison and Dr. Harriet had now crossed the lawn and entered the canteen. Dominic sat opposite a skinny pale man in a keeper's uniform, eating a large pie that was hemorrhaging gravy. The man looked up at Dr May and then across at the new lad accompanying her. Edison saw a brief flash of puzzlement cross the man's face, which then almost immediately, faded into an unnatural smile.

"Hello Dr. May." The man said as they passed his hand in the air. He had a splott of gravy around his mouth and puff pastry crumbs sprinkled down his overalls. The man was obviously a messy eater, although he was so thin, that you would wonder he ever ate at all.

"Hello Bob." Dr. May cheerfully replied as they passed.

Edison then realised that this must be Bob Soup, the keeper who had lost his finger to a pterodactyl as an adolescent.

He looked over at the mans raised hand and could just see the over-sized 'toe' thumb grafted onto his hand, dirty with dry mud, and fingers stained yellow by nicotine.

Bob Soup had worked at the zoo for many years and was regarded as a loyal member of staff, if a little odd. He did have a secret sideline selling premium dinosaur compost, purloined from the zoo. This was so small scale that anyone who knew turned a blind eye. Bob thought of it as a perk of the job, and only made a small amount of extra cash from it, selling to gardening friends and relatives.

Bob looked over at Edison and winked. It seemed a conspiratorial gesture. Had Dominic told Bob about them being inside the Tower, and Edison getting locked in? Dominic was still purposefully looking down into his dinner, and Edison couldn't tell if the two knew each other, or had by chance just happened to sit at the same table.

"Hi Reg," Dr. Harriet said. "I found Edison wandering about. He seemed a little bit lost."

The Director of the zoo had covered for Edison and not mentioned the Walters Tower, he couldn't believe it. He really had thought that he was going to get into trouble.

"Got lost did you?" Reg asked.

"Err, yes," Edison stammered. "Sorry."

"No worries," Reg replied kindly. "Can't expect you to know your way around the whole zoo on just your second day, can we?"

Edison felt awkward and bad about lying like this to Reg. He knew the zoo layout well enough, he studied the map on his bedroom wall most nights, and apart from the secret pathways, he would never have gotten very lost. Edison looked over towards Dominic, who was still deliberately not making eye contact. Reg saw this and must have suspected something, as Dominic had to spent the rest of the day cleaning enclosures, under the supervision of senior keepers.

"Let's grab a quick sandwich." Dr. May said to Edison, as the lunch hour was almost over.

#

That afternoon Reg decided to give Edison a break from cleaning dung and show him some more of the zoo.

"Let's go and see the T-Rex!" Reg shouted excitedly as they left the canteen.

“See you again Edison.” Dr. May smiled. “It was good to *bump* into you.”

Edison couldn’t help but blush a little as he waved goodbye.

They approached the T-Rex enclosure and looked over its low brick wall. Edison looked over the inner wire fence at a small, cat-sized dinosaur, looking up at him. Reg threw it a dead rat and the dinosaur pounced on it. The creature shook the rat in its vicious jaws, sharp teeth quickly ripping through the flesh. Soon the ragged morsel was swallowed and the little dinosaur roared. It wasn't a loud roar, but it was a genuine Tyrannosaurus Rex roar. The smaller dinosaurs were housed in what had once been the original petting zoo, where children would have watched rabbits and Guinea pigs scamper about. Now they could watch meat eating dinosaurs feed on the very mammals that once played here.

The flaw in Dr. May’s method for creating dinosaurs that of their size had proved fortunate in many ways for the original animal zoo. Its Victorian buildings, enclosures and grounds had been built to house nothing larger than bears, elephants and giraffes. There would have been nowhere in its present location to house gigantic dinosaurs, if they had grown to their full scale. Dr. May and the trust would have had to establish a completely new zoo or even safari park, with abundant land, probably outside of the UK.

The T-Rex looked expectantly up at them both, hoping for another tasty treat. Its head tilted to one side like a begging puppy dog, and its green nostrils flared. When it realised it wasn't going to get anything more it spat, hissed, and walked away.

"Moody, little thing," Reg said. "That's one dinosaur I'm glad isn't fully sized!"

Edison had to agree. They looked really nasty, even when moggie sized!

#

Edison couldn't wait to tell Orla and mates at school about his first weekend working at the Dinosaur zoo. He took in his official employee baseball cap to show her. As usual Edison and Orla walked to school that Monday. Most of the time was taken up with Orla chatting about school gossip or what had been on the television last night. She had already lost interest in Edison's job at the zoo having heard as much about it as she wanted. Orla had very little interest in dinosaurs, which Edison believed was one of her few flaws.

Orla's family was of course wealthy enough to take her to the zoo whenever she liked. They had a family season ticket, but rarely visited.

"OK, I will pop in next Saturday," Orla joked. "And wave at you through the bars!"

"But you never go there." Edison said.

"I can smell the dinosaurs from our house." Orla said. "Growling and farting all night, it's not right!"

"But it's the only Dinosaur zoo in the world!" Edison would yet again try and explain. "The only one!"

"Cats are better than dinosaurs." Orla stated, unimpressed.

Redfield's Academy was modern and shiny, and it was unlikely that Edison and Orla would have ever attended the same school, but for the fact that Orla's family had put time and money into helping establish and build the new academy. Orla's parents could easily have sent her to the expensive Clifthill College, if they had wanted. Edison wasn't complaining, the Academy was a great school, it specialised in arts and sciences, with very little sport, so he was happy.

The school week dragged by slowly, and Edison couldn't wait for the weekend to come around. Most of the other pupils at Redfield's were happy for Edison getting the Saturday job, but a few seemed a little envious.

"What did they make you do?" Alfie Strange mocked. "Clean the Brontosauruses big fat bum?"

"Yeah, they had him collecting Dino-do!" Eric Crackle, his spotty friend, chipped in

"It's called dung." Edison wearily replied. "And yes one of my jobs is clearing out the enclosures."

"Bet it stinks." Alfie said.

"We compost it all." Edison explained for the millionth time. "I will bring you a bag in, if you want me to?"

"Nah, you're alright mate," Alfie replied. "But I'll have a free ticket if you can get one?"

Edison had told Orla about his experience of getting locked in the zoo's tower. She knew Dominic as they were almost neighbours. Dominic had even flirted with her once, much to Orla's disgust.

"He thinks he's in some boy band or something, yuk!"

"Stupid hair." Edison agreed.

"I would stay away from him if I were you." Orla warned. "He's a bit weird if you ask me."

#

Alex was being more annoying than usual and Edison thought that he was probably a little jealous. Alex had offered to sell the zoo one of his inept handmade Totem poles, thinking that it would fit well inside the zoo. The crudely carved sculpture would have given many a visitor nightmares and was possibly a health hazard anyway.

Carving wooden sculptures and Totems was one of Alex's more recent hair-brained schemes. The crude hulking objects filled the small communal garden behind their block of flats. Most residents were too scared and intimidated by Alex to complain. What had once been a quiet garden, with flowers and trimmed lawn, was now a noisy mess of wood chippings, old paint cans and precariously balanced carvings. Mandy, badgered by many of the other residents of the flats, had tried to encourage him to take up a new hobby, without much effect.

The disfigured Totems of animal and human heads stood impassively looking into many of the flats windows. More than one resident had been spooked in the middle of the night by the horrible misshapen faces staring in at them, for a second believing that a psychopath with a terrible make-up job was about to climb in and attack them. Babies cried at the crudely modelled animals and had to be swiftly whisked away.

Alex made a small amount of cash from selling his smaller carvings at car boot sales and in lay-bys. These misshapen sculptures of hedgehogs, rabbits, meerkats and deer, were more roadside road kill than cute Disney. Models of emaciated, injured and diseased mammals didn’t sell well. These disfigurations were not done purposely by Alex, he was just an inept craftsman.

When he had approached the zoo with the idea of them commissioning him to make a specially crafted Dinosaur Totem and then displaying it in the zoo gardens, they had graciously declined. This had annoyed Alex who believed his totems to be amazing, highly crafted works of art.

The zoo had thought Alex’s totem poles were tacky, badly made, and quite probably dangerous. They also couldn’t see why the Dinosaur zoo even needed a totem pole. What they didn't realise was that Alex had no idea that early American Indians and dinosaurs hadn't co-existed. Films he had watched in his youth had convinced him that they had all inhabited the same ancient world. Confused memories of watching B Movies, where actor cavemen fought with model rubber dinosaurs, were surely based on historic fact. No one had ever described Alex as being a bright spark.

Alex saw Mandy as a temporary stop gap, and Edison, well he wished he wasn't around. The kid only seemed interested in dinosaurs and fossils, and now he had landed a part time job at the zoo! Edison's bedroom was like a ruddy museum with its figurines, books, and posters on the wall. Alex didn't find dinosaurs interesting at all, unless he could make some money from them, and the fact that the zoo hadn't offered him any, made him angry.

Still Alex had a plan. It was an ingenious idea that couldn't fail, and would land him quite a lot of cash. Now that the kid was working inside the zoo he could start to put it all into action.

Chapter 11
Stealing Secrets.

Jacobi hit the computer keyboard out of frustration. Why whenever he had an important email to write and send did the buildings IT systems go down? He knew hitting the computer wouldn't make any difference but he felt better for it. He had been known to throw monitors at the office wall in a rage before, when something went wrong. Jacobi shut down the computer. One good thing about running a huge corporation was that there were plenty of minions ready to sort out these types of annoying problems.

He sat alone in his large office with its plate glass panoramic view. At his desk, he often felt that he was sitting on air, high above London. The office was starkly furnished with just one huge desk, an expensive office chair, a small leather guest seat and a luxury feather-filled sofa in the corner. Two walls were totally transparent with sliding glass doors opening onto a narrow metal balcony.

The other walls in the room were empty apart from a bookcase and a life-size painted portrait of Jacobi. It was painted about 10 years ago and showed him standing majestically outside his country estate. He loved looking at this picture.

Sitting back in his chair he began to wonder whether the man, 'The Fixer', he was about to email would be ready to take on the job that he had in mind for him? The man's identity was secret and Jacobi would only contact him, requiring his specialist services, when all other avenues had failed.

Jacobi picked up the phone.

"Jane, could you get the IT guy up here? The email has gone down again!"

"Sorry Mr Magnuson, I'll chase him up."

Jacobi put down the phone and stood up. He walked over to the large glass windows and slid open the doors. The sound of traffic and car horns started to fill the room. Even this high up you could hear the traffic. He looked down at the cars and tiny people walking on the streets below.

Jacobi could feel nothing but disdain for them.

"Little ants, that's what you are." He sang out to them. "Tiny, little, squishable ants!"

The phone on his desk rang. It would be Jane ringing to tell him that the IT guy was on his way up. He let the phone ring, and ring, and carried on looking down at the world below.

#

The large bulky man sat and sank into the blue Ikea sofa. He wore a suit, and looked as if he might burst out of it at any moment. His muscular frame, covered in tattoos, filled the fabric. In the army he had followed a rigorous diet and exercise regime that he now tried to stick to in civilian life, but it was much harder being disciplined outside of the army.

On his coffee table sat a small wireless laptop. He had logged on to one of the many unsecured wireless broadband systems in the block. People really could be stupid in this part of London he thought. Here he was using their Internet, and it didn't cost him a penny.

The flat and its utility bills were rented in another mans name, all paid for promptly on-line by a small company based outside the UK. There was no identifiable connection between him, the company, or this flat. Very few people knew his real name. Those that did were either dead or living somewhere under witness protection.

It paid to be anonymous in this game and the clients preferred it that way. It was safer for everyone concerned. Clients knew that they would never be connected to the crimes he perpetrated for them. Sometimes very serious crimes. If for any reason a client withheld a payment, well then they wouldn't know when, or who, would be coming for them, would they? Clients for this very reason always paid up on time. He always took a job on the basis of a 50 percent fee upfront and 50 percent on completion. On the rare occasion when a job couldn't be completed he always wired back the initial 50 percent, deducting 15 percent as an administration fee. This often surprised the client, but he believed in being honest, and it had given him an excellent reputation as a 'Fixer'. Trusting him made the whole job easier. Reputation was everything.

His laptop had software that scrambled his emails and where they were sent from, disguising the IP addresses he hacked into. The software randomly generated locations from around the globe. If anyone should try to track him down via the emails he sent and received they would become very confused, it looked as if he moved about a lot. The software was also clever enough to track and log such searches. He had great pleasure once in telling a client that he knew that they had been spying on him and trying to track him down, and that perhaps they should desist from doing so. This must have scared the bejesus out of them. An apology wasn't necessary, but he did increase their final fee, just for the hell of it.

Today he was waiting for an email from 'Huge Foods'. They had hinted they might have a new job for him last week. He had worked for them in the past and felt it was beginning to be quite a lucrative contract. They always transferred his fee promptly, on time, to his account in Switzerland. Which then, unknown to them, automatically transfer the cleared monies on to two other separate offshore accounts. These would then route the money to the accounts of various businesses around the globe. Such phantom businesses would then pay his bills, credit card, rent, etc. Cash could sometimes be a problem, but he had found that most of the jobs he completed had the added benefit of having large amounts of cash lying about, this he kept.

If you killed a stranger, you might as well take their wallet as you take their life. The people that hired him concerned themselves mostly with stealing secrets, espionage, and digging for dirt on rival companies. Assassination was rarer, but he could, when needed, make any killing look like an accident, suicide or even natural causes.

Since leaving the army five years ago he had made four times the money he had in the whole of his 20 year career. His new life was tax free, lucrative and untraceable. He was earning and saving enough money to retire comfortably by the age of 45, just a couple of years away.

The laptop in front of him pinged. An email from 'Huge Foods' had dropped into the in-box. He read it with glee. A tune came into his head as he got up and went into the kitchen to fetch a drink. He started humming it to himself and remembered it as a song his dear old Mum had sung to him as a child.

He hadn't visited a zoo for years and the idea of breaking into the world's only dinosaur zoo intrigued him. He would pay the zoo a visit in daylight for a recce, to check out their security measures. What was the CCTV like, the locks and alarm systems, the security guards etc. One important thing he had learnt in the army was that it was the knowledge and intelligence picked up before going into battle that counted. Being prepared saved lives.

He knew that the zoo in Clifthill was surrounded by posh housing and parkland, so there shouldn't be an issue of getting inside. The CCTV and alarms might be a problem, but he had dealt with complex systems in the past.

He chuckled and drank a can of ice cold peach tea in one large gulp. He returned and typed a brief reply, emailed it, and closed the laptop lid. He had a quick stretch of his arms and twisted his neck in an arch until it gave a satisfying click. He started to sing.

"We're all going to the zoo tomorrow..."

He walked over to the locked cabinet in the corner of the room and opened it.

"...zoo tomorrow, zoo tomorrow."

Inside was a varied selection of guns and weapons.

"Mamma's taking us to the zoo tomorrow,"

He picked up one of his favourite handguns. It felt cold and heavy in his hand.

"And we'll stay all day."

He continued humming the tune to himself while starting to clean the gun. Would he retire in a few years? - He wasn't sure. He really loved his work far too much.

#

Jacobi looked at his computer screen, but there was still no reply. Outside he heard the distant siren of an ambulance or police car in the hum of the traffic below.

The Fixer at the end of this email was a very bad man, a man who would do nearly anything for money. A nameless soul who was hidden deep, in a dark, secret world. Jacobi knew from past dealings from him that he was expensive but totally reliable. He was a man you could trust, but not one that you ever hoped to meet.

Over the years Dr. Harriet May had been approached by just about every conceivable food business looking to officially affiliate themselves with the popular Dinosaur zoo. Sausage suppliers, kebab kings, burger barons, pork scratching czar's, crisp companies, meat pie producers and the conglomerate Huge Food Inc. All wanted the prestige of being affiliated with the world famous Dinosaur zoo. It was profitable and lucrative having dinosaur themed food products within their business. Brontosaurus Burgers, Stegosaurus Sausages, Prehistoric Pies, and other dinosaur themed meat treats, filled many a shelf and supermarket aisle.

Huge Foods and the other manufacturers knew that they could shift more products with the celebrated official Dinosaur zoo logo printed onto their packaging. Dr. May and the zoo had so far resisted all offers. The zoo was profitable in its own right and didn't need any such sponsorship. The food manufacturers where frustrated that the zoo and its worthy director didn't want its famous logo supposedly tarnished and sullied by their products.

Jacobi and Huge Foods had become more and more frustrated with her reluctance to licence the zoo's branding. Jacobi was particularly annoyed with Dr. May, who over the years had refused all invites to meet with him and discuss what he believed to be mutually beneficial arrangements. Such a unique deal, if he could make it happen, would help propel Jacobi to the position of Huge Foods World chairman, pushing his rival Bob Black off the top spot.

He had tried to orchestrate 'casual' meetings with the zoo director at charity fundraisers and the openings of various prestigious buildings. Dr. May had been polite opening it. The message was a simple, 'OK'. There was an attachment with the email, a small video link. Jacobi clicked on it and a colourful film popped up. It seemed to be an excerpt from an old children's television show. The video showed a bearded man, playing a guitar, and surrounded by jolly children. He was singing them an upbeat song, about a zoo.

Chapter 12
The Lost Cat.

The weeks passed with Edison alternating between weekdays at school and weekends working at the zoo. He now worked most Sundays, when he wanted to, which he always did. The long summer school holidays were just around the corner and Reg Green had asked him if wanted to work a few extra days at the zoo. Edison had of course jumped at the chance.

"We get really busy over the summer." Reg said. "So the more staff about, the better."

"I get bored during the summer holidays." Edison replied. "We never really go away anywhere."

"Well the work will be a bit more interesting, not all cleaning and sweeping. You might even get to sell some ice creams too!"

Edison didn't mind what the work was, as long as he didn't have to spend time with Dominic. The two had kept away from each other since the incident in the tower. They had of course bumped into each other in the staff room, canteen and around the zoo, but Reg had intuitively given them different jobs to do. Dominic was looking more confident and cocky then ever. Because Edison hadn't dropped him in it, he somehow felt tortoises, using tough 'beak' like mouths to methodically slice and rip through their food.

A couple of Stegosaurus was usually the first to arrive on stage to warm the audience up. They would come out and rummage for the fruits and goodies, hidden earlier by the keepers. They moved in a slow, but humorous fashion, but sometimes waddled surprisingly fast across the stage, and this would always make the younger audience giggle. The Stegs would occasionally pause from eating, and look up at the audience, momentarily curious at all the faces looking back at them.

It had also been known for a stubborn one to get stuck half-way between the scenic cave backdrop and the stage, not wishing to go forward, but also unable to turn back. It would then take some coaxing and pushing by the keepers to get the creature unstuck, and back inside, much to the audiences delight.

The grand finale of the show would often be a display by Ted, the zoo's favourite pterodactyl. This magnificent creature was ten years old and one of the few pterodactyls that could be handled. It had been hand reared by Reg and the keepers when it was a sickly youngster, rejected by its siblings. Now an adult it was about the size of a large macaw parrot.

Ted was a male and so had a brightly coloured crest and a wonderful blue iridescent wing membrane. He also had large sharp talons. The keepers wore thick gloves with a metal chain-mail core to handle him. Ted mostly spent his time eating flying insects and fish inside the Pterodactyl enclosure. Coming out into the main part of the zoo, to fly about, was a real treat. He surprised the audience with his entrance, by climbing and pulling himself up over the back of the stage backdrop. The audience would draw breath as they first saw his long talons reach over the edge of the set, followed by his reptilian body as it popped over the top.

The pterodactyl had been trained to screech on command and open his huge wings once he reached the peak of the display. This always made the audience gasp and reduced some of the smaller children to shock and tears. All were amazed at how the sunlight reflected and sparkled off his huge wings like liquid steel.

Ted would then either hop off, or glide down, onto the stage and walk about. Reg or one of the other keepers would then stretch their arm out and the pterodactyl would jump into the air and land gently onto the outstretched gloved arm. He would be rewarded with a small fish, which would be eaten in one swift gulp. Up close Ted's wings had a rough texture not unlike pine-cones and he emitted a scent of oily fish. A smell most of the keepers had gotten used to.

Edison dreamed of the day that he might be able to hold this creature and let it take a fish from his fingers. The closest he had gotten to the pterodactyl was when he had been alone and vulnerable, up in the oak tree, and at the time that had seemed threatening. He could now see that Ted was about as tame as a prehistoric creature could get.

As the grand finale to the lunchtime displays the keepers would lift their arm and the pterodactyl would flash open its wings and rise up into the air. The audience would always cheer as it started to glide into the sky above their heads.

The pterodactyl would do a wide loop, flying around the grassy picnic area, the visitors looking up in awe. For a second everyone had the same thought, 'Would it come back?' Then, in a silent and elegant manoeuvre Ted would glide down and return to land on the keepers outstretched arm. The air would fill with spontaneous clapping and cheers of delight from the relieved audience.

#

Life at home had been becoming progressively worse since Edison had started working at the zoo. His Mum was really happy for him and so proud that she told everyone about his amazing job. Alex however seemed worse than ever. He had started drinking more and the neighbours had started to complain because of his terrible taste in music. Alex only seemed to own one album, 'The Best of the Wurzels', and when drunk he would play the song 'I am a cider drinker', very loud and repeatedly. He drunkenly sang along, annoying everyone in the block.

Mandy had little control over him at moments like this, and not wanting to provoke an argument, she generally let him get on with it. They would turn the CD off when Alex drunkenly fell asleep. Edison generally kept to his room and tried to ignore the racket downstairs. He would wear his headphones to drown out the noise and draw or read.

It was on one such night that Orla texted him to say that one of her cats, Yul, was missing. The cat had gone out earlier that afternoon and not returned.

'WILL U HELP ME FIND IT?' Orla texted.

'OK.' Edison typed back.

He looked at the dinosaur clock illuminated on his wall. It was Ten thirty. Mum wouldn't want him out this late, so he would have to sneak away.

'OUTSIDE UR HOUSE IN TEN MINS.' He texted.

It was a warm night so he only put on a checked shirt over his t-shirt. He picked up his trusty torch and opened the bedroom door. Downstairs yet another awful rendition of 'cider drinker' rang out. He could see from the top of the stairs that the living room door was partly closed. He would sneak by and quietly exit the front door. He knew Alex was in the living room but wasn't sure where his Mum was.

He tiptoed down the stairs knowing that no one would hear the odd squeaky stair as he went. At the end of the corridor he saw his mum in the kitchen. Luckily she hadn't seen him. He crept towards the front door, opened it, and slipped out.

The air outside was summer fresh and he could feel latent heat radiating off of the buildings brickwork. He ran down the steps to the road and towards Orla's house. He found her sitting on the garden wall.

"I brought a tin of pilchards." She said, as Edison approached. "Yul loves anything fishy."

They spent an hour walking the streets, looking and calling for the lost cat. Edison's fingers became sticky and smelly from waggling wet pilchards under bushes, inside dustbins, beneath parked cars and anywhere else they could think of.

Orla tapped the open tin can with a fork and called the cat's name.

"Here Yuliee, Yuliee," She sang. "I've got some fishy-fish, fish-fish for you!"

They did discover two cats that weren't Orla's. One had been a very persistent tom that kept following them, attracted by the scent of seafood. They had managed to lose it a few roads away.

"Do you like pilchards Eddie?" Orla asked.

"Not really."

"No one does do they?" Orla stated. "Except cats," She paused, "And otters!"

Edison looked confused.

They had arrived back outside Orla's house, her cat still at large somewhere.

"I better get home before Mum realises I'm missing." Edison said.

"Thanks for helping anyway Eddie." Orla smiled. "I'll let you know if Yul comes home."

"Night." Edison waved as he walked home. Orla had palmed him off with the smelly tin of pilchards, asking him to throw them in the nearest litter bin, if he passed one. Why she couldn't have put them in her own dustbin he didn't know.

As he approached the flat he could hear terrible music still pumping out of the living room window. He dumped the half empty can of pilchards into a large wheelie bin, that when opened, smelled awful. He slammed the lid shut quickly. It was then he heard a plaintive meow. A small fur-less cat sat cowering under a bush at the bottom of the steps. It was Yul, Orla's bald cat.

"Here Kitty-Kitty." Edison felt stupid beckoning the cat and wished he still had the can of pilchards in his hands. The cat didn't seem inclined to approach him.

"It's me, Edison. Orla's friend." Edison approached the cat but it took fright and darted up the steps, just as the flats front door opened and light spilled out. Alex stood at the door, a drink in his hand. The cat darted up the last few steps and into the open doorway, passing between Alex's legs.

"What's bleeding going on?" Alex shouted.

"It's the cat. Orla's cat. It's been missing!" Edison explained.

"What, your posh girlfriend?" Alex leered.

"She's a friend, *not* a girl friend." Edison replied.

"Yeah, Yeah." Alex said. "I can't stand bloody cats, so get it out now!"

Edison ran up the steps, and could smell the alcohol and stale fags on Alex's breath as he tried to pass. Alex made a drunken joke of blocking the doorway, but eventually he moved out the way, to let Edison in.

Chapter 13
The Key.

Edison rang Orla early the next morning and told her that he had found her cat, which was now safe in his flat. He had wanted to text her the night before but Alex had kept him up late into the night explaining his plan.

Orla appeared at the front door carrying a wicker travel cage for Yul to go back home inside. She hadn't been to his flat that many times before, and Edison always felt a little embarrassed when she came around. Compared to Orla's family mansion their flat was modest and tiny.

His Mum always kept the place clean and tidy, but Alex had done a great job of messing it up during the night. Beer cans and general rubbish littered the floor. Alex was now thankfully passed out in bed. His snoring was audible even in the kitchen. How did his Mum ever sleep through such a racket Edison wondered?

"Why is Yul in the bin?" Orla asked, concerned.

"It was the only way I could catch him." Edison lied.

He couldn't very well tell her that his drunken step dad had dropped the poor thing in again.

Orla opened the flip top lid and looked inside.

"Hello Yuliee." She said kindly. The cat gave a plaintive meow and stretched its legs.

"Do you want to come out?"

Orla reached inside and lifted the poor cat out and cuddled it close. The cat purred in appreciation.

"Did nasty Edison put you in the bin?" She asked the cat, who meowed back.

"I couldn't help it." Edison implored. "I did put some blankets in to keep her warm."

"Where did you find her?" Orla asked.

"Err, I got up early this morning to have a look around again."

Orla wasn't really listening; she had started to put the cat into the wicker cage. The happy cat turned around inside, settled down and purred.

"Let's go home." Orla said through the bars to Yul. "I'll open you a special tin of Tuna chunks!"

Edison opened the door for them and Orla skipped down the steps.

"Bye Orla." He shouted after her, but couldn't be sure if Orla returned his goodbye or not. He stood at the top of the steps in the open doorway and felt the morning's cool air on his face. The road was quiet and deserted. It was still very early as he had called Orla as soon as he thought she might be awake. He felt tired and a little annoyed, even though he had found her cat, Orla was obviously peeved at him.

He closed the flats front door and locked it. In the kitchen he drank a glass of water and cleared up some of Alex's mess. He now really wished that he hadn't agreed to Alex's idea. But if he hadn't he didn't know what Alex would have done to the cat next. He had a mean streak, and kicking the bin may have only been the start. Alex would probably have thrown the poor thing out of the window if he felt like it!

What Alex wanted wasn't good. He needed an easy way to gain entry into the zoo at night. For this he wanted a security pass key. Edison didn't have one, and knew that it would be trouble trying to get one. He could fob Alex off for a little while, but eventually he would have to steal a pass from the zoo. It could only lead to bad things.

"Get me a key or I will make the rest of your life a bleeding misery." Alex shouted at Edison, throwing an empty beer can across the room.

"They don't have keys! They use plastic swipe cards and only the full time staff has those!" Edison explained. "They have their photos on and everything."

"Well steal one of those then!" Alex shouted. "And get me the pass code as well."

"You want to burgle from the zoo, don't you?" Edison cried. "I'm not going to help you do that, it's wrong. I'll get the sack!"

"I only want to go in and have a look around, when nobody is there." Alex replied.

Edison thought perhaps Alex intended breaking in and robbing the place.

"It'll be a quick in and out. No one will ever know."

"Don't be stupid. They have cameras and security." Edison explained. "They will see you on the CCTV!"

"I'll worry about the cameras." Alex said. "You just get me the key card."

Edison really couldn't believe that this was the deal he had agreed to, just to free Orla's stupid cat! He had promised Alex that he would get him a key.

"I don't know the pass code." Edison told him truthfully. "What good is the card without the security number?"

"Have a look for it around the offices." Alex said. "Someone is bound to have copied it down somewhere."

"I hardly ever go into the offices." Edison pleaded.

"You're good chums with that Reg Green, have a look on his desk." Alex said. "He looks stupid enough to have it written down".

Edison would have liked to punch Alex for insulting Reg like that, but thought better of it. They argued like this until Alex ran out of beer and went to bed. Edison had no real choice but to steal the key card. That probably didn't matter too much, as all the cards had personal identity photos on them, not Alex's ugly mug, and they were useless without the pin number. Alex would find it hard going breaking into the zoo with just the card and no code, and Edison wasn't going to give him the code, even if he did come across it.

#

It turned out that finding a zoo pass key was easier than he expected. During the first week of the summer holidays he was asked to help clear out the locker rooms and staff kitchen. It made a change from sweeping dinosaur dung and in comparison it was a much easier job. The locker room, unlike the rest of the zoo, rarely got cleaned. Pieces of lost clothing, ancient newspapers, magazines and rubbish lay forgotten about inside disused lockers. Edison even found a rock hard sandwich, green and half eaten on top of one cabinet. He scooped this and all of the other rubbish into a very large black bin which he dragged and slid around the room.

On top of one of the lockers was a pile of abandoned clothing, gathering dust. It looked to have accumulated there for months. As he pulled at the dusty bundle something fell to the ground. It was a battered key card, dirty, but still in its plastic holder. Someone had obviously forgotten to take it off when they threw their old clothes on top of the locker. Edison smiled when he saw who it had belonged to, Bob Soup, the keeper with the bitten off finger. He knew Bob Soup couldn't be missing the pass as he still worked at the zoo and must therefore have a replacement one.

Edison quickly hid it in one of his dungaree pockets and continued to clear up. He would give the old pass to Alex and they would then be square. Edison doubted that this old key card would even still be activated, as Bob would have a newer one. Anyway it wasn't his problem. If it didn't help Alex burgle the zoo then that was a good thing.

He certainly wasn't going to sneak around Reg's or anyone else's desk, looking for the security code. He would tell Alex that he had searched, but not found a thing. He knew that Alex would be more than happy with just the key card anyway.

"Alright lad?"

Edison jumped as Reg entered the room.

"How's it going?" Reg asked.

"Good, thanks." Edison replied, feeling a little nervous knowing that he had the stolen key card in his pocket.

"Found anything, interesting?" Reg asked.

"Err, no." Edison worried that Reg might have somehow seen he had found and taken the key card. "Just an old sandwich."

"Really?" Reg replied excitedly, "Pass it here."

Edison looked slightly confused, but started to reach down into the black bin, now overflowing with rubbish.

"Not really lad." Reg Laughed. "I'm just pulling your herring!"

Edison looked up at Reg's big smiling face and couldn't help but grin back.

"I did wonder." Edison chuckled.

Edison went home that night feeling guilty about having the stolen pass key hidden in his pocket. He decided that he needed time to think and so wouldn't give it to Alex straight away. The pass could easily be hidden in his bedroom somewhere. Perhaps Alex would forget about their deal and the whole thing would pass over? Edison doubted this, but it was worth waiting to see what happened.

babbling school party, he saw Bob Soup emerge from behind the trees. The keeper looked worried.

#

That night at home Edison was confused by what he had witnessed that day. He was sure that he had never seen the huge stranger at the zoo before, yet one of the keepers seemed to know him. Who was the odd man and why was Bob Soup meeting him in secret?

Edison had seen the stranger taking photos and drawing plans of the zoo in his notebook. It was all very suspicious. Perhaps he did work for the zoo in some capacity? That would explain Bob knowing him, but didn't really explain the man's rudeness. Edison felt the part of his head where the man had tapped him. It was bruised. The man was very strong, that was for sure.

The book Edison was reading was a thriller set in a museum. He had found it in a box of old books his Mum had ready for taking to the Charity shop. The paperback was old and tatty but the illustrated cover garishly depicted a Egyptian mummy coming alive and attacking visitors. It was a great cover. He thought that he was probably too young to be reading such a book, but it made a change from dinosaurs.

Alex came thumping up the stairs, whistling. Edison heard him go into the bathroom and turn the radio on. Edison could still hear him having a pee over the radio football commentary. The football crowd cheered just as Alex flushed the toilet and left the room. The light switch pinged on in the bedroom next door as Alex farted on the landing. 'Nice' said Edison under his breath.

"Thanks for this!" Alex shouted, putting his head around the door.

Edison looked up from his book and saw Alex's grinning face. At first he was confused as to what his Step-dad was on about. Alex was waving something in his hand. It was the zoo key card Edison had hidden in his bedroom a couple of days ago. Alex must have been sneaking about his room while he was out all day. Edison thought that he had hidden the card well and really hadn't wanted Alex to get his stupid hands on it.

"You were going to give it to me, weren't you?" Alex grinned. "That was the deal, right?".

"Err, yeah." Edison stammered.

"Sure you were!" Alex added sarcastically. He tossed the card in the air and caught it with his right hand.

"Thank, umm," Alex said reading the name on the key card, "Mr Soup for me."

With that he darted out of the room and ran down the stairs laughing. He heard his Mum downstairs ask Alex what was so funny but didn't hear the reply.

'Great' Edison thought, now Alex had a chance of breaking into the zoo. He didn't believe that just the key card would get Alex in, but he still felt troubled. Even if Alex only got caught trying to break into the zoo it was bound to lead back to Edison. The police would easily link the stupid criminal to his step-son, a lad who just happened to work at the zoo. The suspicion would fall on Edison as having been the person who purloined the key. No one would believe that he really hadn't had a choice.

noticed. He followed behind, making little noise, creeping along the pavement. From a distance he had seen Alex pass silently through the staff entrance, with ease. He had obviously used the key card, but where had he managed to get the code from?

Earlier Edison had spoken to Orla on the phone and told her the whole sorry story. To his surprise Orla was actually quite shocked and had agreed to help, if she could. Edison thought she must have felt a little guilty, as it was her stupid cat that had started all the trouble in the first place. If Edison hadn't needed to rescue the cat from Alex he wouldn't have had to make the deal with him concerning the key card.

"Eddie!" A voice whispered from across the road.

He looked across and saw Orla crouching down at the corner, hidden in the shadows. She had been as good as her word, saying she would meet him outside the staff entrance. He felt a great sense of relief, knowing that he wasn't on his own lifted his spirits.

Edison ran across the road and crouched down next to Orla.

"He's just gone in." He whispered.

"I know." Orla replied. "I thought he couldn't get in without the alarm code?"

Their plan had been to stop Alex from attempting to break into the zoo. They hadn't fully formulated how, but thought that they might be able to alert the zoo security, who would scare him off. Maybe they could find an alarm to set off, or ring the door bell for as long as it took to raise the security guards.

"He must have got the code somehow." Edison explained. Alex knew a lot of the local criminal fraternity. He might have been able to get it from them.

"What shall we do?" Orla asked.

It was a good question, and one that Edison didn't have an answer for at the moment.

#

That night's storm seemed to be picking up energy and getting closer. Flashes of blue lightning momentarily lit the interior of the empty office. The thunder shook the wooden walls, and Alex thought that he couldn't have picked a more perfect night to rob the zoo. Any noise he made would be put down to the storm by the security guards on duty. He had noticed that all of the zoo's CCTV cameras and much of the exterior lighting wasn't working. The storm had probably caused a localised power cut, shutting down parts of the zoo's security; it all certainly worked in Alex's favour.

The office was in the main administration block and it was here that Alex hoped to find the zoo's weekend takings and petty cash. There would be a strong box or possibly a safe hidden somewhere in the room. Outside rain had started to pour down, drumming heavily onto the offices cedar roof tiles. The warm summer night was starting to turn decidedly wet and chilly.

Alex crept through the office opening desk draws and rifling through metal filing cabinets. He didn't feel the need to rush, as he doubted the lazy security guards would want to come out in this weather. Poor fragile things wouldn't want to get wet now, would they?

Suddenly a flash of lightning lit the sky and Alex caught a glimpse of movement outside the room. The dark shadow of a man cut across the window. Somebody was standing just outside the office door. Quickly Alex crouched down behind a desk. A crack of thunder filled the air and then silence. Alex hid quietly behind the desk and wondered if he had been mistaken and imagined the figure. Had zoo security seen him enter the office and now come over to investigate?

He then heard a noise just outside the office door. A small torch beam momentarily lit up the textured glass panel. Someone was trying to pick the lock from the other side. The torch momentarily lit the glass again and Alex saw the silhouette of the dark figure. A security guard wouldn't need to be so clandestine, and pick the lock, thought Alex. So who was it?

The metal lock catch clicked and silently the door began to open. Alex could see very little from where he was hiding behind the desk. A sliver of white light from outside sliced into the room as the door opened. Alex saw the large figure of a man slip stealthily into the room and carefully lock the door behind him.

#

Outside the zoos' thick stone walls Edison heard the night sounds of the dinosaurs within. The approaching storm seemed to have made them more vocal than usual. Sleepy grunts and high pitched screeches cut through the air. Orla was also looking nervous about the storm. Maybe the reality of going into the zoo, at night, now seemed a bad idea.

Edison felt guilty that he had even asked Orla to come along with him tonight. It was his fault that he stole the security key card. Why hadn't he hidden it better in his bedroom or not taken it home in the first place? Edison hadn't had much choice, true, but now he wished that he had stood up to him more strongly.

They would now have to follow Alex into the zoo and try to persuade him not to do something stupid. Perhaps they could sound an alarm that would flush Alex out before he stole anything. It was risky, and Edison certainly didn't want to get caught breaking into the zoo himself, but he couldn't think of any other options.

"Stay here Orla." Edison said. "Keep a look out and ring my mobile if any police arrive."

Orla was crouching under a bush, both to stay hidden and also get some cover from the first drops of rain. She looked relieved that Edison wasn't insisting that she go into the zoo with him. They both checked that their mobiles were on and ready.

"Good luck." Orla whispered, giving him the thumbs up.

Edison first tried the door that Alex had used, thinking that he may have wedged it slightly open, to make his escape easier later on, but it was locked solid. Edison then wondered if one of the best ways into the zoo could be via the cafe. The Claws Cafe sat elevated above the gardens, but did have stairs and a service lift

The guy finished putting the books back into place. This was Alex's chance; surprise the intruder as he left the office, and steal the backpack. He moved carefully out from behind the desk, ready to spring. He held tightly onto the small, but solid fire extinguisher, ready to smash it into the mans face.

The head torch bobbed towards him moving for the door. Alex sprang up, and with a huge roar, swung the metal extinguisher into the man's huge head.

The intruder yelled in surprise as the extinguisher bounced off his head, and clanged to the floor. The head torch flew across the room, it smashed and broke, and the room was thrown into darkness. Alex blindly reached out to where he had last seen the backpack, hanging off the intruders shoulder. He miraculously grabbed it first time and ripped it away. In a flash Alex was at the door and pulling at the handle. The door wouldn't open.

'Oh shit', thought Alex, as he frantically pulled at the handle, clutching the backpack. Behind him he heard the grunts of the intruder who was now fully aware that he had just been robbed. Being hit hard in the face with the fire extinguisher had momentarily knocked the man off his feet, but now he was getting back up.

Alex frantically felt about in the dark for any type of catch on the lock. He regretted that he hadn't had a good look at the inside of the door when he broke into the office earlier.

He remembered the click of the catch, as it automatically locked itself, when the intruder had closed the door. Alex's hand found this and turned it quickly. The door swung open wide. He felt the air behind him move as the stranger made a grab for his shoulder and missed. Alex flew out of the doorway and was running down the corridor, his feet thumping along the wooden walkway, past dark and empty offices.

At the end of the passageway he came to the top of the stairs that led down to the zoo. He heard the intruder following closely behind. The man was fast for such a large guy. Alex ran and jumped two steps at a time down the stairway, but in the dark he misjudged the last couple of runs, and slipped on the wet wood.

He fell winded onto the wet gravel covering the ground. In the dark he could just make out the rest of the zoo before him and knew that he must escape and hide as soon as possible. As he started to pick himself up, he felt a heavy thud on the ground nearby. Instead of running down the steps after Alex, the intruder had simply jumped over the walkways barrier, and landed with a angry grunt.

#

Edison was still looking out at the administration block when a light came on over the office door. The door flew open and Alex came running out. The light was movement activated, and Alex really was moving very quickly. Maybe he had just set off an alarm inside or something? Edison couldn't really hear much behind the thick glass which was now obscured by rivers of rain. Alex had looked spooked that was for sure. As he bounded away down the wooden walkway someone else came running out of the office. Was it a security guard? Edison couldn't see from this distance but the large man was dressed in black rather than a guard's uniform. The stranger chased after Alex, who was now off down the staircase. Edison couldn't be sure but it looked as if the pursuer had jumped into the air and vanished, both men were now out of view.

He knew that now was probably a good time to leave. Alex had been spotted and would no doubt be captured. Edison didn't want to get caught too. The rain was getting heavy and a clap of thunder overhead didn't make the idea of trying to find Alex in the dark and wet very appealing. Orla would be waiting outside and he didn’t want her getting into any kind of trouble. Alex would just have to fend for himself now.

Edison ran back towards the kitchen and the open skylight. He looked up at it, large drops of rain splashed through the gap and into his eyes. The skylight was about 8 feet up and out of reach. Edison was only five foot three inches tall; there was no way he could jump up to it. He would need to find something to stand on. A block wood chopping table in the corner of the room looked promising. He gave it a push but it didn't budge. It must be bolted to the floor or wall. He quickly checked and found all the other kitchen units securely fixed also.

At the back of the room was a series of large storage cupboards recessed into the wall. Edison opened one up and found a group of stacked chairs. These would do. He took a couple and placed them below the skylight. On tiptoe he would just be able to reach the lip and pull himself out. He ran back for two more, to gain a little extra height, but it was too late, the zoo's alarm system had just started to scream into action.

#

Alex could just make out the man's silhouette in the zoo's dim lighting. The huge man loomed before him like an angry bear standing on hind legs. Rain bounced off his body and it actually seemed to steam into a halo of mist around him. There was no way, Alex realised, that he could fight this man and win. He would just have to outrun him and hide.

"Drop it!" shouted the stranger, his voice so deep that it sent a chill through Alex's spine. This was no ordinary Clifthill burglar. The man took a step towards Alex just as the zoos alarm system screamed into action. Instantly Alex used the distraction and was up and running away towards the maze of enclosures.

He ran beyond the closest dinosaur pen towards the more wooded jungle and picnic areas. Here he would easily be able to hide amongst the dense vegetation. The jungle area had huge Ferns and Gunnera plants and he intended to become invisible beneath them. Alex wasn't an idiot; he knew that this man would make mince-meat of him, if he ever caught up with him.

The zoo had many secret exits and passages that the keepers used for deliveries, shortcuts and moving the creatures about. Alex had heard about these hidden walkways that ran around, and even under the zoo, off limits to the public. If he lay hidden long enough, the intruder would eventually leave, and he would be able to search for a secret exit, and escape.

He dived into the jungle area, crashing through spiky undergrowth and damp ferns. He ran deep into the vegetation until he felt sure he was well hidden from his pursuer. The alarms here didn't sound so loud and piercing. He sat down in a patch of wet leaves and put the stolen rucksack between his knees. He opened it and like a blind man used his inquisitive hands to investigate the interior of the bag. His heart lifted as he fingered what felt like many envelopes stacked with cash. Without knowing it, what he was holding was more important than money. These contents of the bag put Alex's life in very real danger.

Chapter 16
Sunday Night Carvery.

Alex had been hiding in the jungle area for over twenty minutes and the rain was still pouring down. He had however remained remarkably dry huddled under a giant Gunnera plant. The alarm system that had been going off in the distance was now silent. Perhaps zoo security had captured the huge stranger? Alex hoped so. The bloke was a giant and he really didn't want to bump into him again tonight.

It was pitch black here so he still wasn't sure of all the contents inside the rucksack. He had found a small metal torch, probably the intruders, and he used this to investigate the other contents. There were definitely a few thick envelopes stuffed with money, but also some unusual bundles of A4 documents, folded in half. A plastic box contained some shiny round computer disc's that looked intriguing. He was chuffed about the money, and would investigate the discs further when he got home, but first he had to find a way out of the zoo, without being seen.

He stood up, wiped himself down and cautiously left the cover of the bushy, dense foliage. He stuck to its outer edge, just in case he stumbled into anyone, and had to duck back in. He hadn't heard any police sirens, and

its fleshy head crest back and showered Alex with hot stinking saliva. The thick spit flew straight into Alex's shocked face, the smell making him retch. Alex stumbled back as the creature let out another screech and an even bigger shower of smelly phlegm. Some blobs of spit flew into Alex's shocked and screaming mouth. He slipped and fell onto his back frantically using his hands to wipe off the thick sticky saliva. Alex started to retch and vomit, and though he tried to move out of its way, much of his own sick fell back down onto him.

"Ahh!" He screamed rolling over as the dinosaur let out yet another burst of projectile greasy mouth gunk. This time it missed and landed on the ground. Alex instinctively picked up a rock and threw it at the cage. It bounced off of the wire, but distracted the dinosaur enough for Alex to get to his feet and move away.

The smell of the stinking dinosaur phlegm and the vomit on his face made him hunch over and retch all over again. Doubled over he could just hear the sound of approaching footsteps. The spit had blurred his vision and with his stinging eyes he could just make out the hulking form of his pursuer coming towards him.

"Shit!" Alex exclaimed, spitting bitter dinosaur juice out of his mouth.

"Give me the rucksack!" shouted the man.

"Look I don't know who you are or what you are doing, but I shouldn't be here either." Alex said, still wiping his face and spitting out gunk. The intruder looked amused.

"It's not funny." Alex cried. "That frigging thing just spat all over me."

"That," Said the man. "Is the least of your problems."

He moved slowly towards Alex.

"Give me the rucksack." He repeated.

"Look, here, have it." Alex said. "I just came to get my hands on some computers and stuff."

The intruder let out a mocking laugh.

"A ruddy thief!" He said. "I hate thieves."

"What are you then?" Alex asked.

"Don't compare me to you." The man's bulky frame came closer. "You're just thieving scum!" He prodded Alex with a thick finger, nearly pushing him over. "Pass me the bag, slowly."

Alex stepped backwards keeping his eyes on both the spitting dinosaur and the intruder. Thankfully the dinosaur had lost interest now, or run out of spit, and had hidden once again in its enclosure.

"Look, let me wipe this mess off." Alex held up the rucksack and gave the man a nervous grin. "Maybe we can split the contents?"

The man said nothing and just kept walking slowly towards Alex, his huge body blocking out any light coming from the zoo. Alex stumbled backwards feeling very afraid.

"Here, have the bag!" Alex panicked and started to take the bag off of his shoulder. "I don't want any trouble".

"Trouble? You look nothing but trouble." The man pushed Alex sharply in the shoulder, making him fall over. The rucksack fell onto the ground landing next to him. The huge man looked down at his hand and saw that it was now covered in Alex's vomit.

"You filthy scumbag!" The man wiped his dirty hand against his trousers and took something out of his jacket pocket.

"Give me the bag!" shouted the man, who was now pointing a gun at Alex.

#

Edison ran down the kitchen stairs and out into the dark zoo gardens. He hadn't managed to get up to the skylight and decided that he would probably have a better chance of escaping the zoo via one of the many secret pathways. He now knew these routes well, and even in the dark he felt he had a good chance of getting away unnoticed.

There was a lull in the storm and the thunder seemed to have passed over. The zoo was still dark and only half of its lighting seemed to be working properly. He took out his mobile phone and sent an emergency text message to Orla; 'GO HOME NOW! URGENT!'. He hoped that the zoo alarms would have scared her off already, but if not, the text would do the trick. He realised that he could use his mobile as an emergency torch. He turned up the brightness and the bluish white light lit his face, making him squint a little.

Edison didn't see any security guards as he ducked down a narrow pathway, and ran along the back of a series of enclosures. He made his way towards the back of the zoo where he knew there was an old disused gated entrance, near to the composting area. This had been used many years ago but still had the small wooden Victorian ticket office beside it. The gates had been locked and covered with thick wooden boards, and was now used as an advertising hording, so he knew that he wouldn't be able to open these. The old ticket hut now doubled as a store room. The keepers kept a range of spades and forks and a couple of rusty wheelbarrows inside. If he could climb up onto the sloping roof, he would then be able to hop over the zoo wall, and down on to the street below. If he couldn't get up onto the roof then he could at least hide out in the shed for the night. This would be cold and risky, and he didn't want to do it, but it might be his only option.

He ran to the end of the pathway, crashing through bushes, his mobile phone helping to illuminate the way. He knew that he would have to make his way towards the jungle area. This would mean crossing over a patch of well lit grass, and one of the zoos major walkways, with all the risks of being seen by someone. He paused for a moment wondering when to make a dash for it.

Suddenly he heard a very loud bang and jumped. Somebody was shouting as a figure ran out from dark shadows, only meters away. It looked like Alex. Edison nearly called out to him but was stopped by the sight of a huge man appearing from out of the dark, chasing after him. Edison recognised the man instantly as the stranger he had been talking to a few days ago. The giant man who had poked him in his head and later been seen with Bob Soup. What was he doing here? Did he have a gun? Perhaps the zoo's night security team now carried weapons?

Edison watched as the two men ran towards dense vegetation and disappeared from view. Was that really a gunshot Edison had just heard? It sounded like one. He had obviously only heard them in films and on television before, but this sounded so much louder. Edison had no idea what trouble Alex had got himself into, but he now knew that he would be of no help to him. The man pursuing Alex was obviously dangerous and armed with a gun. The night security guards must be all over the zoo looking for the burglars, Edison couldn't be found as well. If caught he was sure to be instigated in the crime, he had to get out now!

#

Suddenly both men heard the sound of approaching footsteps. Someone was running towards them, and it looked like they had a torch. The huge man was distracted for just a moment. Alex didn't wait for a better opportunity. He sprang to his feet and lunged himself at the stranger. The gun in the man's hand exploded, and a bright flash blinded them, as they toppled backwards. Alex felt like he had just slammed himself into a breeze block wall. He had hit the man hard, but the force only managed to make him lose his balance. The big man's foot had, fortunately for Alex, slipped and skidded on a patch of fresh vomit, helping to knock him over.

Alex was off and running, the rucksack slung tightly across his shoulder. He didn't know where he was going, he just ran blindly, as fast as he could, into the night. The alarm system was on again, loudly bouncing around the zoo. He guessed that the gunshot must have at last roused the security guards from their slumber.

He ducked cautiously behind bushes, leaves brushing against his face in the dark. He hoped to be near the perimeter of the zoo. He came to a arched doorway. He took the small pocket torch out of the rucksack and read the sign on the door, 'Private - Employees only'. He tried the handle, but it was locked. Maybe he could force the door? The wood looked dry and old. He gave it a swift kick, but nothing budged. Next he ran at it, using his shoulder as a ram, the door cracked somewhere. Another few shoulder blows should break it, he thought. The door must lead to a way out of the zoo, he hoped. He heard something in the distance. Footsteps were running toward him. Alex managed to give the door two more solid jabs and it sprang open. He fell through into darkness, the torch landing onto the ground, and illuminating part of what looked like an underground passageway.

It felt damp and musty in here, the floor gravelly and wet. Stringy vegetation hung down from the curved stone roof and drops of water dripped onto him. Alex picked himself up, grabbed the torch, and ran down the dark tunnel. His legs feeling wet and stiff.

He looked back over his shoulder only to see the large dark silhouette of his attacker framed in the tunnels entrance. It looked like a scene out of a horror film as a bolt of lightning illuminated the sky outside. Alex kept running, not knowing where it might lead. The torchlight frantically bounced around the interior of the tunnel as he ran. He didn't dare turn the torch off and be plunged into compete darkness.

The passage wasn't straight, so he kept banging into the wet slimy walls, as the tunnel curved left and right. His cold hands got cut and grazed, searching for

the many private access conduits used by the keepers, enabling them to move dinosaurs and deliver food.

"Where are you? - Thief!" shouted the man.

Alex hid as best he could and wondered what the hell he was going to do? He was trapped, with the huge man directly in front of him and a mass of angry looking dinosaurs clumped around the only escape route. He didn't know much about the specifics of the different dinosaurs, but he knew enough that most of them were vicious, with sharp teeth and claws, and could inflict a terrible bite. Some could even be venomous, with poison not unlike a snake.

The air was suddenly filled with a high pitched yelping and hissing. The little creatures weren't very happy at having intruders in their home. Their alarm call sounded urgent and spooky, bouncing around the enclosure, in the dark. Alex watched their tiny bright eyes, as they moved their heads about in a rhythmic wave. He could feel their hunger and keenness to attack.

Alex took the small torch out of his pocket, turned it on, and threw it in the direction of the stranger. It passed over the huge mans head and landed in a thud below the gang of dinosaurs, illuminating their reptilian bodies. The man turned as the torch passed by and came face to face with more than thirty snarling Segisaurus, each the size of a large domestic cat, huddled angrily on the rocks.

Caught off guard, the assailant stepped backwards, away from the tunnel entrance. One of the Segisaurus launched itself off the rocky outcrop and jumped onto the man's solid shoulder. Immediately it sank its razor sharp teeth, into the man's thick muscular neck. He screamed in shock as the needle fangs penetrated his skin and instinctively brushed the creature off. The dinosaur landed on the ground next to his feet. The stranger began to violently stamp on its small splayed body, and Alex heard the sound of its bones snapping like brittle twigs. The creature's pitiful cries increased the agitation amongst the others in the pack, who watched from the safety of the rock face. The huge man rubbed at his neck where the creature had bitten him. He looked at the blood, now running down his neck, and staining his hand.

"Sod it!" He exclaimed angrily. He turned back towards the place that he had last seen Alex.

"Rucksack, now!" He screamed. "Or you really are a dead man."

With his back now turned towards them the Segisaurus started to launch themselves off the rocks in small groups. They landed in huddles on top of the man's head, back, and shoulders. Their razor teeth and cutting claws piercing and slashing at his skin. Alex could see bloody gashes appear on the man's face as he struggled to move away, with at least fifteen of the creatures attacking him. They viciously hung on to him as the huge man turned in circles using his flaying arms to try and prize them off. The man's cries chilled Alex to the core; he couldn't imagine the pain these creatures must be inflicting.

Now was his only chance. Alex sprang up, and in the darkness, ran frantically towards the escape door, past the mass of violent slashing and ripping. The screams of pain in the air propelling him along as he jumped down all of the steps and landed heavily against the wooden door. A sharp and painful jolt passed through his shoulder, but he couldn't stop now.

Quickly he pulled at the door, it wouldn't open. A bolt of pain, like an electric shock, shot through his hand. At first he thought that he must have touched one of the electric fences but then he looked down and yelled, a Segisaurus was hanging onto his arm by its teeth. Alex vigorously shook his body and thumped the creature hard against the door frame. The Segisaurus came flying off taking a chunk of his upper arm with it.

Again he pulled at the heavy door; conscious of the huge mans frantic screams behind him.

The door was locked.

How could it be? Alex slammed his shoulder into the damp wood and pulled as hard as he could against the handle. He could hear the small dinosaurs jumping and landing onto the ground behind him. He didn't dare look around. With one final enormous effort he pulled the door open.

Alex ran through the door, instinctively slamming it shut and sliding the rusty bolt as best he could. His heart pumped heavily in his chest and fear caused him to collapse to his knees. He crumpled to the floor as the screams within the enclosure became more muffled and distant.

The heavy door rattled and Alex could hear bumping against the other side. Other Segisaurus must have followed him as he escaped out of their enclosure. They smashed their bodies against the door, snarling and scratching at the old wood, trying to get through. His arm was stinging; the creature had managed to bite through his shirt, and deeply into his flesh. The wound felt almost numb now; perhaps the creature had injected anaesthetic venom as it bit into his flesh?

Alex ran in the cold darkness down the tunnel, hoping to find the exit. Short, sharp, thuds continued to rattle the door in its frame. The dinosaurs persistent attack on it was the last thing Alex heard as a creeping blackness seeped into his mind, smothered it, and he fell unconscious into the wet gravel.

Chapter 17
Monday Morning.

He was woken by the clatter of a passing lorry, its heavy wheels disturbing gravel on the road. The stationary car shook as it passed by and he heard the sound of tiny pings of grit hitting the sides of the doors. Alex got up from the back seat of the car and looked out the window, his face illuminated by the orange of a street light. The windows were steamed with condensation and he had to wipe it away to see out. It was still early, stars still present in the dark morning sky.

His head hurt and his body ached a lot, sleeping in the back of the car had been uncomfortable. His arm throbbed and stung like crazy where the dinosaur had bitten him. He looked down at the injury. A row of sharp teeth had cut into the flesh and the wound still looked raw and bloody. His arm felt stiff and weak and his hand had swollen up. It felt numb, as if he had been sleeping on it all night, stopping the circulation.

It better not be infected, he thought. He remembered a nature programme where it said that a Komodo dragon's mouth was so full of bacteria, that if one bit you, and you survived the attack, you still might die from the bite anyway. The germs in the dragon's filthy mouth would infect the wound and kill you slowly later. It was even thought that they might inject unique, skin rotting, venom when they attacked.

What of the dinosaurs that had attacked him and killed the stranger? Their mouths must be full of bacteria and other filthy stuff. He had poured a can of cola into the fresh wound, hoping, to clean it. The fizzy bubbles had stung like crazy and he had to stop himself from nearly crying. He had then made a makeshift bandage, out of a torn sleeve ripped from a shirt, he found in the boot of the car.

Alex had been lying low all night, hiding. Crunched up in the back of the car, parked down a narrow side street, near the zoo. He had stumbled upon it, parked amongst a row of others, after having escaped. Luckily for Alex the car door had been unlocked and he had simply jumped in. It probably belonged to a rich student who couldn't be bothered to lock it. There was a dirty blanket on the back seat which he had used to cover himself, both to stay warm and hidden. He had slept fitfully, the screams of the huge stranger still in his thoughts and disturbing his dreams. Alex knew that he was lucky to have survived and not died the same horrible way.

What had happened in the zoo that night still confused him. First he had escaped the huge nutter who had first attacked him in the office. Then, thankfully, he had gotten away from those vicious little dinosaurs. The things had swarmed onto the other man like land based piranha. The huge man had never stood a chance as they massed over him. They had probably ripped him to shreds long before Alex gained consciousness.

and reach up to the metal guttering, levering himself up to the parapet. The roof was steep and wet from the rain and he slipped on the slimy brown tiles. Thankfully he had regained his footing, though the wet algae and damp moss on the roof made it hard not lose his footing and slide off. Slowly he started to climb up to the peak of the roof, on all fours like a monkey. At the top he grabbed onto a cold metal weather vain and pulled himself up and over the smooth curved ridge tiles. He scrambled onto the other side and started to carefully shimmy himself down.

Two sharp metallic anti-intruder razor spikes ran along the external wall below him, complete with lines of barbed wire wrapped around them. Thankfully for Edison these had been positioned to keep intruders out, not in, and so had been situated just under the lip of the buildings roof. Anyone trying to break in here, with a ladder from the outside, would have been confronted with the vicious looking defences and given up.

If he was careful as he jumped he would miss any of the spikes and barbed wire. He lowered himself gingerly over the roofs edge, his hands grabbing tightly onto the only thing he could, the slimy guttering. His fingers felt frozen already and having the tips of them immersed in the ice water flooding the gutters didn't help.

He hung down over the wall and dropped down to the dark road below. The fall was more than he'd expected, but he'd landed fine.

As soon as he got into his bedroom he texted Orla. He really wanted to call her but was worried that her mobile going off so late at night would attract attention.

'ARE U OK?' He texted and waited for an answer. He then crawled into bed fully clothed and exhausted. He relaxed and looked up at the ceiling. The phosphorescent plastic stars he had stuck up there last year, glowed bright, greenish white in the dark. If you squinted your eyes it was almost like looking up at a real constellation of stars in the night sky. On his bookshelf three illuminated dinosaurs stood sentinel in a row, watching over him. Edison was really glad to be home, safe in his warm bed. He started to drift off into sleep.

Suddenly the mobile phone beeped under his pillow. It was a reply from Orla.

"HOME SAFE. NEED SLEEP. TALK 2MROW."

Edison texted an 'OK' back and felt relieved that Orla had got home safely. He shouldn't have let her come along in the first place; it had been a stupid idea.

He slept deeply for a while until a nightmare startled him awake in the middle of the night. He was running in loops inside of the zoo. He continually ran around, and around, repeatedly, in a cartoon, speeded-up way. A mad gunman was chasing after him. Every time the man fired the gun a small firework shot out from it and popped into the night sky. It was the same stranger he had seen chasing Alex, now pursuing him, and laughing wildly like a hyena.

Edison woke up Monday morning feeling tired and exhausted. It was still the summer holidays, so he was able to laze in bed, until hunger drove him down into the kitchen. He wouldn't be working at the zoo again until Wednesday. So would have to wait until then to find out the news about the break in. Reg was sure to fill him in on all of the details. He may be lucky and here some gossip before then but he doubted it would make the local news.

As he went downstairs, still in the clothes he had been wearing the night before, he really hoped not to bump into Alex. Alex was sure to be home by now, full of arrogance and cockiness at not having been caught. Hopefully he had gone out already? Or still be lying in bed himself.

The kitchen was empty and Edison helped himself to a bowl of cereal. 'Dino Choc Rocks', the ones with mini white marshmallows dotted between various dinosaur whole wheat shapes. He gulped this down with a glass of milk and a over ripe banana. The nights adventures had made him really hungry and his stomach rumbled in appreciation. In a moment he would call Orla and arrange a meet. They needed to discuss last night and get their stories straight. It was unlikely anyone even saw them near the zoo, but just in case they needed to agree a plan. Perhaps they could say that they had been out, but looking for one of Orla's cats? His Mum would kill him if she found out that he had been wandering the streets late at night anyway.

He was just putting the dirty cereal bowl into the sink when his Mum walked in. She looked tired and her eyes looked a little red and puffy, from crying perhaps.

"Alex didn't come home last night." She told him flatly.

Chapter 18
The Secrets in the Safe.

"Edison," Reg called from the kitchen. "Dr May wants to see you in her office."

It was Wednesday morning and Edison had just arrived at the zoo. He was just putting on his zoo uniform in the staff locker room. Today was his first day back after Sunday night's robbery. He had been feeling nervous about coming in today anyway, thinking that he would be under suspicion in regards to the break in, and now Dr May wanted to talk to him! It couldn't be good news. Had they caught Alex? Was that why he hadn't been home for the last few days? Did the police have him in custody? Had he dropped Edison in it?

Too many questions, best face the music, and get it over with.

"Just coming." he shouted back to Reg.

The two of them walked silently up the steps to the admin offices and Reg knocked loudly on Dr. May's door.

"Come in." Dr. May shouted from within.

Reg opened the door for Edison and he walked into the office, Reg following behind. Edison felt his legs begin to shake as Dr. May looked seriously up from her desk.

"Edison we have a few questions to ask you." She said.

"Have a seat son."

Edison turned to see for the first time, another man standing in the corner of the room. He was stocky with short brown hair. He took an orange plastic pen out of the breast pocket of his checked suit and tapped it against a small notebook.

"This is Detective Williams," Dr. May said to Edison, "He's here about the robbery."

Edison felt faint and hot. He could feel his whole face starting to blush.

"Hello." The detective said walking toward Edison and shaking his hand. "Have a seat lad. I just need to ask you a few questions."

Edison sat down in the chair opposite Dr. May's large desk. Reg sat at the back of the room. Edison hadn't seen his face but guessed he must be looking very annoyed. He really had let Reg down. He could almost feel the keeper's eyes burning into the back of his head.

The detective had stepped to the side of the desk and was looking thoughtful.

"As you probably know by now, we had a break in on Sunday night." Dr. May explained.

Edison shuffled awkwardly in the plastic seat.

"They didn't take much. We think the alarm system scared them off." Dr. May continued. "Regrettably our CCTV system wasn't working."

"Most likely the storm." Detective Williams said. "There were a few localised power cuts that night."

Edison felt relieved. At least none of Sunday night was going to be caught on camera. Therefore there wouldn't be any footage of him or Alex inside the zoo.

"Although there were some signs of possible tampering with the security system." Dr. May explained.

The Detective looked over slightly annoyed at the zoo's director. He probably hadn't wanted that nugget of information to go public.

"Yes, perhaps." The Detective said. "Now Edison we feel that you might be able to help us with some of the mysteries of the break in."

'Oh no!' thought Edison, they knew something. How? He felt a bead of sweat run from behind his ear and down the back of his neck.

The room went silent for just a few seconds, but it felt like days. Everyone in the room was looking in Edison's direction.

"There was a man, Ed." Reg said, breaking the silence.

"Sorry?" Edison replied, momentarily confused, turning to look in Reg's direction

"We checked the last few weeks CCTV." Dr. May explained.

"And we found footage of a large stranger visiting the zoo." The detective continued.

But if Bob was innocent why hadn't he turned up for work the last few days? And where was Alex?

"Cheer up Ed, it's not the end of the world!" Reg laughed as they walked down to the zoo.

Reg was right, and Edison could have jumped for joy, his relief was so great. He had thought that he was going to lose his job when they first called him into the office, but it seemed that, thankfully, no one had even the slightest idea that he had been inside the zoo on Sunday night.

#

Dr. Harriet May put down the telephone and sat quietly at her desk. She wasn't sure who had broken into the zoo and burgled her office. They had certainly been clever and organised, the zoo's CCTV and alarm systems had been tampered with, and the contents of the safe stolen. She doubted that anyone would be caught; the police scenes-of-crime officers hadn't, as yet, found anything. There was some evidence that a possible struggle had taken place in the office. A small fire extinguisher had small traces of blood on it, maybe from being used as a weapon? DNA evidence might prove useful later. It was all very confusing. Perhaps the thieves had a falling out and tried to double cross each other?

It was a professional job and Dr. Harriet guessed that espionage, industrial or otherwise, was involved. Someone must have offered Bob Soup a lot of money to be involved. Bob had been a loyal member of staff for many years, it didn't make sense that he would now turn against the zoo. He must have known that his key card would be recorded as having unlocked the staff entrance on the Sunday night.

The large stranger in the CCTV footage didn't look like an ordinary burglar. He seemed more like a soldier, with his careful planning and military bearing. A lot of thought had gone into breaking into the zoo and only someone with experience would have been able to crack the safe.

Over the years Dr May had been approached many times for the secrets to her research. All sorts of people would make a lot of money if they could replicate her results and so create dinosaurs. Rival scientists, other zoos, food companies and even the government had contacted her in the past. She always gave the same answer, that for now, the zoo's research was private and not for sale.

She would of course now increase the zoo security systems, as a show of taking Sunday's burglary seriously. She didn't want anyone thinking that her research methods would go unguarded. A more up to date camera system and another emergency generator, for future power outages, should do it. They would do their best to make any future break-ins a lot more difficult. How the intruder had escaped the zoo that night was still a bit of a mystery. There were plenty of places inside where someone could jump the wall to get out. No doubt the large stranger had designed his escape route while he was doing the recce of the zoo. She would get Reg to have a look around and see if he could find any clues.

Dr. Harriet felt remarkably calm about it all, and had predicted something like this would happen sooner or later. She knew a time would come when someone would manage to get their hands on the contents of the safe. So she had filled the safe with decoys. All of the contents were illusions of the real thing. None of them were genuine or authentic. They just looked like they were.

The paperwork and computer discs were worthless fakes of the real thing. Tiny nuggets of truth encased in a mass of pseudo science and bullshit. It would take anyone researching these a very long time, and a lot of money, before they realised that what they had was gobbledygook. She had produced a mad, yet convincing, replication of her methods. Did they really think that she was stupid enough to leave the real secrets in the zoos safe?

In the past she had quietly let go employees who, she realised, had been planted into the laboratories, just to gather knowledge. All of this espionage was carried out subtly and she dealt with it in a low key way. Over the years she had made it an open secret as to where she kept her research. Now that the safe had been so expertly broken into, the individuals that had organised its theft had shown their hand. She looked forward to hearing about failed dinosaur experiments and research on the scientific grapevine.

Whoever had stolen the information was in for a long hard, and ultimately disappointing, year or so. Dr. Harriet smiled to herself, confident in the knowledge that what had been stolen was nothing of any use. She had already replaced the stolen items, with more fake research, in the safe. You never knew when the next break in might occur, and now that this last one would be talked about as a success in the underworld, someone was bound to try again soon.

The telephone call had been from another idiot offering to sell her the stolen information back. She had already had four similar calls since the break in. Whether these people were actually in possession of the stolen goods or not she wasn't sure. It didn't matter and the police could deal with all of that.

No one, not even her brother Hadley, knew the whereabouts of her real research. In some ways she rather liked the idea of the secrets dying with her. Perhaps one day she would leave a series of letters, instructions, and her papers to be handed down to a trustworthy heir. Reg was possibly that person. He was devoted to the zoo, but he was also older the Harriet. He might pass away before she did. Hadley would probably sell the secrets to the highest bidder if they ever came into his possession. He wasn't a bad man, and she loved her brother dearly, but his interest in the Dinosaur zoo was purely monetary.

Until then she would keep up the pretence of hiding the secrets in the safe. If anyone wanted to steal her work then they would be naturally drawn there first. It was a good ruse. She had initially got the idea from a television detective show where a rich widow supposedly kept all her jewellery in her bedroom safe. Naturally anyone wanting to steal her jewels would head there. This was the logical place for storing valuables after all, and she did in fact leave some minor pieces of jewellery inside. If the safe got broken into, these items would be stolen and the thief would leave reasonably satisfied. However the rich widow cleverly stored the bulk of her jewellery elsewhere. In the detective show it was hidden in old paint cans, in her boathouse, at the bottom of the garden.

Dr. May liked these slights of hand. She hoped to always play games of distraction, and stay two or three steps ahead of her rivals, and her enemies.

#

As they walked over to look at one of the enclosures, Edison really wanted to ask Reg more about the break-in. What had been stolen was still a mystery. There had been a rumour of a large sum of money, the zoo's weekend takings, being stolen. Edison was careful not to ask Reg too many questions, but he wanted to know what had happened to Alex. But he had to be careful and not seem too interested and possibly then incriminate himself.

Reg led him over to the enclosure and lent against the railing.

"I tried to give them their midday feed yesterday." He told Edison. "And they turned their noses up at it. Usually they love an old goat carcass."

Edison looked down into the enclosure and the Segisaurus, 'The Sid's', did look a bit lack lustre. They lay about, huddled in groups, sleeping and farting. Normally they would be running around in the mornings, fighting and sniffing the air for food.

"They have been off their food for two days now." Reg explained.

"It could have been the storm." Edison said.

The summer storm had spooked all of the creatures in the zoo. The Apatosaurus had produced a lot more dung than usual, possibly because of fright, brought on by the thunder and lightning.

"The whole compost area does seem twice as big as usual." Reg remarked.

They both looked at the small deer carcass laying in the wheelbarrow, its legs upright and rigid, pointing to the sky.

"If I had known better," Reg said. "I would have said that they had eaten already!"

"It must have been the thunder." Edison replied.

"That or they have been attacking each other again." Reg said.

Edison looked concerned.

"When we went in and cleaned the enclosure yesterday, we did a head count." Reg explained. "And one of the Sid's was missing!"

It was well known that many of the dinosaur species fought each other for supremacy and over food. Sometimes they could also turn cannibalistic, but this was rare. The storm must really have put them all on edge that night.

"It couldn't have got out." Reg explained. "So it must have been eaten!"

Edison helped Reg tip the dead deer into the enclosure via one of the feeding gates. They watched as a few Segisaurus slowly got up off the ground and went over to investigate it. There didn't seem to be any urgency in them wanting to eat anything. The dominant pack leaders sniffed the carcass and climbed over it, the sharp claws on their back feet digging into the deer's rough hide. Eventually a small group of Sid's started to use their vicious teeth to rip open the stomach of the deer. They certainly looked to have the beginning's of a healthy appetite now.

"And look at this!" Reg said, holding up what looked like a badly chewed leather army boot.

"I found this in their enclosure. Some idiot must have chucked it in over the fence!"

Edison looked at the large boot swinging from Reg's hand. He recognised it as the type of boot the huge stranger had been wearing the other day. Could it have belonged to him? And if so, what was it doing in the Segisaurus enclosure?

Chapter 19
Life after Alex.

For the following week Mandy and Edison had no idea where Alex had disappeared to. The robbery at the zoo seemed to have blown over, so why hadn't Alex returned to the flat? To Edison's great relief no one had established a connection between himself and the break in. The burglary remained unsolved and the mysterious stranger was the main suspect. There had been a rumour of blood and DNA, but it obviously couldn't have been Alex's, as the police hadn't come knocking at their door. No useful fingerprints had been found at the crime scene, the CCTV was non existent and the intruders had vanished.

Alex must know by now that he wasn't under any suspicion? Edison thought. He would have seen that the CCTV had been inactive that night, due to the storm, so there was no video record of him being there. Alex must have escaped after the robbery, as the grounds had been thoroughly searched by the police, and no trace of the intruders was found.

After a couple more days Mandy had registered Alex as missing. The police hadn't seemed too concerned, as he was well known to them as a local criminal and general pain in the backside.

"I wouldn't worry." The tallest of the uniformed policemen told her when they visited. "I'm sure he'll be back."

"He's not gone off like this before." Mandy explained to them.

"Is it possible that he may have found someone else?" The other policeman asked.

"Sorry?" Mandy sounded annoyed.

"Well he's a bit of a charmer, old Alex, isn't he?" The Officer continued.

Mandy knew that Alex was a bit of a rogue, but as far as she could tell, he hadn't found another lover.

"What if he got drunk and had an accident?" Mandy asked. "He might have fallen in the river or something."

The policemen said this was unlikely; there had been no reports of anything odd being found in the river. They left taking a recent photograph of Alex and saying that they would be in touch.

Edison listened to them from the flats window as they left.

"Good riddance." One of them joked, as they got into their police car. Edison heard the other policeman laugh as the car drove off quickly, its radio blaring out a bad rap song.

The flat felt much more like 'home', and much more relaxed without Alex around. Edison had to admit that he hoped his step-dad wouldn't be coming back.

Perhaps, he thought, the policeman was correct, and Alex had found someone else? He wouldn't have put it past him. Alex had always been secretive, and if he had gotten away with the zoo's takings, the first thing he would do is go away and blow it. No doubt he was hiding away somewhere, spending it all.

At first his Mum was a little sad and blue, but thankfully she soon began to get angry. Edison discovered her having a major clear out of all of Alex's possessions. First she tipped out all of his clothes and shoved them untidily into black bin bags. She left these at the bottom of the steps, outside the front of the flat, ready for the charity collectors to pick up.

Even though Alex had lived in the flat for two years, there were few other items. Mandy collected what she found and stuffed them all into old cardboard boxes. She then shoved these into Alex's stupid car, parked just down the road. It was surprising that he hadn't taken the Fiesta, as it was his pride and joy. The car keys were still hanging up in the kitchen. Perhaps he was too shamefaced or embarrassed to show himself at the flat to pick up the keys?

Mandy had contacted one of his 'mates' at The Spoon café. She told him where he could find the car and collect it and its contents. The mate sounded genuinely concerned about Alex's disappearance, but Mandy knew the crowd who frequented The Spoon were all dishonest scumbags. Thieves, liars and crooks the lot of them. If they *had* known where Alex was, and *who* he may now shacked up with, they wouldn't have told her anyway!

To the neighbours' great relief Mandy then organised for the communal gardens to be cleared of Alex's junk. She had found a small stash of cash Alex had hidden in the bedroom while clearing out his stuff. She took great pleasure in using some of this to pay for a couple of burly blokes, with a van, to cart the whole lot off to the dump. The half finished totem poles, paint cans and other old bits of Alex's junk would all be going.

Alex had unknowingly paid to have his crummy rubbish taken away and crushed. It was more than he deserved, thought Mandy. Soon all traces of Alex were gone. The flat and garden looked great and Edison suspected that there was now no way Alex would ever get his feet back in the door.

One solitary totem pole remained standing upright in the garden. This was the largest and most complete, and the removal men hadn't been able to take it away. In his wisdom Alex had incompetently, but solidly, concreted its base into the lawn. No one liked it, with its crude carvings and messy paint job. It gave many of the residents the creeps, staring as it did into some of their windows.

"Sorry," One of the tattooed blokes told Mandy. "We'll need a chainsaw on this one."

His shaven headed mate stood next to the totem, giving it a good push, making it wobble ominously.

"We could just force it over Rick!" He told his friend.

"Too risky," Rick replied. "Might go straight through one of the windows or something.

The two agreed to come back at a later date with a borrowed chainsaw and cut it down. Mandy agreed, the totem would have to stay for a little while longer.

"Scary thing, innit?" Rick said as they drove off, looking up at the gaudy totem. Both men couldn't wait to chop the whole thing up and sell it as firewood.

Edison was so happy to have his Mum back to her happy, Pre-Alex self. Her confidence had returned and he couldn't believe it when she announced the next morning.

"Let's go to the zoo!" Mandy exclaimed. "You can show me around."

Edison couldn't have been more chuffed. As an employee he had free entry whenever he liked, and a family pass. He would give his Mum a guided tour of where he had been working all summer.

He took her to the zoo early, it was a day he wasn't working, and they had a great time. Edison proudly introduced her to Reg Green and some of the other keepers he knew.

"Good to meet you 'Edison's Mum'." Reg joked as he vigorously shook Mandy's hand.

"Hello Reg." Mandy smiled back. "I feel I know you already, Edison never stops talking about you!"

After the mornings tour Reg treated them both to lunch in the staff canteen. Edison watched as his Mum laughed as Reg entertained her with amusing zoo stories. Edison hadn't seen his Mum this happy for years. She even looked younger. Reg went on to tell her about how well Edison was doing at the zoo and what an excellent member of staff he had become. Edison couldn't help blushing as his Mum looked on proudly at him.

"Right lad, let's go and see what today's slop is." Reg laughed as he slapped Edison on the shoulder.

"Don't worry." Edison said to his Mum. "The foods really good here."

The three of them got in the queue, each sliding their wooden trays along the metal counter.

Just as Edison thought that today couldn't get any better he looked up at the chalkboard menu behind the warm metal counter. Today was 'Pie, peas and mash' day. Edison really didn't think life could get much better than this.

#

Jacobi had been waiting a over a week now for any contact from The Fixer. So far there had been nothing. No emails, mobile texts, phone calls, absolutely nothing. He had been expecting a package, sent special delivery, in the post. It hadn't arrived at the London offices. It was all very strange. The man seemed to have completely vanished.

Huge Foods still had its contacts within the Dinosaur zoo, and they had confirmed that a break in had taken place on the Sunday night as planned. The zoo's security had been professionally tampered with, the safe expertly opened, and its contents stolen. The robber or robbers had escaped, and so far there were no suspects. So what had happened?

The Fixer was still owed the last fifty percent of his fee. The agreement being that the money would be immediately transferred into his bank account on confirmed delivery of the contents of the safe. It didn't make sense that the safes secrets had been successfully stolen but not delivered into Jacobi's hands.

All Jacobi could do is wait patiently for an answer. He had sent the man emails, what more could he do? His plans to oust his rival, Stephen Black, would have to be put on hold for a little longer.

Jacobi knew that the robbery would never be traced back to Huge Foods or himself, but this wasn't his greatest worry. What if the Fixer had planned all along to keep the contents of the safe, and sell them on to one of Huge Foods many competitors? Could that be possible? It just seemed so unlikely. The man was a pro, with an excellent reputation to hold on to. He had never let them down in the past. Why would he want to now go behind Jacobi's back and lose any of Huge Foods future business? It didn't make sense.

The telephone on his desk ran.

"Yes?" Jacobi answered abruptly.

It was Jane his receptionist.

"I'm sorry to disturb you Mr. Magnuson, but I have Bob Black on the line for you."

"Oh God, what does he want!" Jacobi remarked.

"Jac, how are you buddy?" Stephen Black immediately came on the line, his American informality irritating Jacobi already.

"Stephen! Fine, fine. How's it going in Chicago?" Jacobi asked as pleasantly as he could.

"Get with the program Jac. I'm in London." Stephen sarcastically laughed.

"London?" Jacobi asked, momentarily confused.

"In fact I'm standing downstairs in the very foyer of this building." Stephen replied.

'Shit' Jacobi thought.

"Come down. I have a car waiting outside." Stephen continued, "We have a few things to discuss."

"What things?" Jacobi asked, but Stephen Black had hung up on him.

#

"We had a message from our insider, at the zoo." Stephen Black explained. "Bob. Bob Soup."

"Soup?" Jacobi asked.

The two men sat in the back of a large black limousine, one of the companies many expensive fleet vehicles. A chauffeur sitting upfront, segregated behind a tinted glass privacy screen, drove them slowly through London's rush hour traffic. Jacobi had no idea where they were heading and Black hadn't bothered telling him.

"Come on Jac, wake up. We've had him on our payroll for years." Stephen Black said looking down at a folder of papers.

Jacobi knew who Bob Soup was very well. He had only talked to him a few weeks ago to arrange a visit between himself and The Fixer. Jacobi had wanted Soup to give the man information about all of the security measures in place at the zoo. He had contacted Soup just after the break in, to see if it had all run smoothly, but hadn't thought to call him recently.

"Mr. Soup is worried Jac." Stephen Black explained. "He's worried about the robbery. The robbery *you* helped organise at the zoo!"

"Where is he?" Jacobi asked.

"He's safe. We have him hidden for now." Black replied.

"Hidden?"

"The man's house was ransacked, Jac." Stephen Black explained, "It seems someone other than just the police is after him."

'Shit' thought Jacobi, Stephen Black seemed to know all about his plan to steal Dr. Harriet May's secrets from the zoo directors safe. But Jacobi still hadn't received anything from the fixer. Perhaps the man had gone above Jacobi's head, directly to Stephen Black? Did Black now have the contents of the zoo safe?

"Where are we going?" Jacobi asked.

"The airport." Black replied. "I'm taking you back with me to the US."

Jacobi looked worried and was about to speak but Stephen Black interrupted him.

"Huge Foods needs the whole situation to be smoothed over." Black smiled like a crocodile, "To go away."

Jacobi sat back in the limousines luxurious leather seat, resigned to what fate might bring. Black seemed to know everything and the fixer was missing. Jacobi had no option but to go along with Stephen Black. As for the future, when they touched down in America, he would have to think of something. There must be away to get himself out of this mess?

Chapter 20
The Water World.

Edison's summer holidays were coming to an end, and in a weeks time he would be back at school, for the autumn term. He would miss working at the zoo during the week. He had become fit and healthy from the extra work and really felt part of the team. He would much rather have stayed working at the zoo than go back to school.

The zoo break-in and robbery now seemed a long time ago. No one suspected Edison of being involved. Alex still hadn't returned to the flat, and that made life at home much more enjoyable. Even his Mum seemed happier. Edison really hoped that this was the last they had seen of Alex.

Today was the first time that Edison had been allowed to help out in the zoo's huge aquariums. He was mainly there to gain experience and supervise, and wouldn't actually be going into the water tanks himself. A day in the zoo's 'Water World' was Reg's treat to say a thank you to him for all the enclosure cleaning and dirty jobs that he had been doing as a trainee. The two had grown close over the summer and Edison respected Reg immensely. Reg himself seemed excited being with the water based dinosaurs that day.

“I don’t often get to work in here myself,” Reg explained, “Not my specialism really.”

A couple of experienced scuba divers had already lowered themselves into the tanks murky water. The Mosasaurus, ‘The Moser’s’, that usually inhabited this aquarium had been moved out to another nearby. Reg and the aquarium keepers had used food, as bait, to coax the creatures into the holding bays.

One of the divers gave Reg the thumbs up and slid beneath the surface of the water. His black wet-suit disappearing as he began his descent and submerged into the murky liquid.

"Rather him than me," Reg said, "Never was much of a swimmer."

"Are they hired to clean just the tanks?" Edison asked. He knew that the zoo didn’t have its own team of divers.

"They work for a specialist cleaning company." Reg said. "As professionals they know more about diving than any of us. We just have to make sure that the aquariums are empty, and safe for them to enter."

The Dinosaur Water World, was one of the most popular and exciting realms within the zoo. The public were able to walk through the exhibit via a series of domed glass tunnels. The glass walkways actually passed beneath and within the huge aquariums, giving an excellent view of the dinosaurs swimming inside the tanks. The aquatic creatures could be viewed swimming around and above the public’s heads. Rocky underwater caves and caverns complete with rocks and seaweed, gave the world a realistic marine design. Sand and soil covered the floor of the tanks. Darting shoals of fish and other water creatures swam inside, both as a source of food, and physical activity for the prehistoric creatures.

The divers went down into the tanks with squeegees and wipers, looking every bit like underwater window cleaners. They only entered the water when all of the prehistoric creatures had been moved safely out of harms way. It would have been deadly to work in the aquariums with the dinosaurs still swimming around them.

"OK Reg, that's both of them in." One of the aquarium keepers shouted.

Edison remembered being here just a year ago, on a school trip. At first he had been a little unimpressed. The light levels were low and you could see your own reflection in the glass tunnel walls. To see the underwater world better he had cupped his hands against the glass and looked out into the murky depths of the water. It was hard to focus on anything in particular in the gloom. Little pieces of floating silt, swirling in the water, and the occasional small fish, passed by.

A shiny fish had darted by out of the gloom, pursued by a large Ichthyosaurus. The creature was the size of a large dolphin, and its huge mouth, full of razor teeth, was heading directly towards Edison's face. At the last minute it turned to avoid crashing into the glass tunnel wall and its tail smashed into the walkway. Edison jumped back startled, and fell down onto his bum. Some of the other kids in the school group laughed.

"Wow!" Edison cried excitedly.

"Coward!" Eric Crackle shouted, laughing loudly, as Edison picked himself up off the floor.

Edison watched as the bluish-grey Ichthyosaurus pursued the fish, twisting and turning, like a dolphin, streams of tiny bubbles trailing behind it as it cut through the water. It was soon out of view, gliding effortlessly into the distant gloom of the tank. Edison couldn't see if it caught its prey or not, but swimming like that he guessed that it must have.

The glass tunnels needed to be cleaned regularly for optimum visibility. Over time algae grew on top of the glass and silt, churned up by the dinosaurs swimming, and settled on its domed surface. The zoo had tried various dirt repellent gels and films on the glass over the years. These worked to a degree, but the walkways still needed a manual clean regularly. Dinosaur poo, scraps of uneaten fish, and rotting vegetation tended to make the aquarium water a bit messy.

The aquariums had been cleverly designed to look as if all the different underwater dinosaurs co-existed within the same tank. They where in fact, separated by thick sheets of glass, almost invisible to the casual observer. These walls prevented rival creatures from mingling and attacking, injuring or even eating each other. Accidents had happened in the past, and some species had occasionally managed to invade a rival's tank, but generally the Water Worlds design and construction worked well.

Rocky islands with sandy and pebble beaches grew out of the water giving the creatures land to bask on. These islands could be viewed by visitors, via a jungle pathway that hung above the tanks as platforms, weaving between the enclosures.

Edison's life had really improved over the summer and the few extra days work at the zoo had helped him gain confident. At the zoo he and Dominic still kept away from each other, as it suited the both of them. Edison still felt annoyed at being locked in the tower, but he realised that if Dominic hadn't locked him in, then he would never have been rescued by Dr. May. Today however both lads would be working along side each other in the water world. Edison had decided to play it as cool as possible. Both nodded heads in acknowledgement, as they met Reg on the gangway, high above the aquariums.

The divers had been underwater for 15 minutes and it was Edison and Dominic's task to pull up the diver's heavy plastic buckets. Both boys wore yellow rubber gloves that kept their hands dry and clean, but kept slipping on the wet rope. As they pulled, water poured out of the plastic mesh built into the base of the buckets, gradually making them easier to lift. The buckets were overflowing with green goo, which smelt really terrible. Edison tried hard not to think of what the gunk consisted of. The buckets plastic mesh allowed the water out, but kept the debris in. Edison tipped the rotting muck out and into a large heavy-duty builder's sack that would be dragged later to the composting area. The empty buckets were then lowered back down into the tanks for the divers to fill.

The two of them had to be careful, perched as they were, on the gangway, high above the water. From here they could look down into all of the separate tanks. Each area would be cleaned in sections, one empty tank at a time. The marine dinosaurs, having been moved out, by opening the sliding glass doors, and letting them swim into the holding tanks. Underwater the glass partitions became invisible. It took a lot of courage for the divers to get in, when you could see the prehistoric creatures, stare hungrily from the other side of the glass screens, sizing you up for their next meal. Edison knew that he couldn’t do it.

It was one of the keeper’s responsibilities to stand above the water tanks and keep a careful eye on the creatures below. It wasn't unheard of for some of the agile creatures to jump up high out of the water, and launch themselves into another tank. This is when accidents could happen and creatures injured from fighting. Reg Green and a couple of other keepers kept a careful eye out for the divers and on the creatures in the water with them.

Out of sight of Reg, Dominic dangled a handful of stringy green slime in front of Edison's face, drops of stinking water spraying into the air.

"Stop it Dominic, it stinks." Edison said angrily.

"Stinks? Must remind you of home then!" Dominic taunted.

One day Edison would devise a way to get back at him, but at the moment he couldn't think of how to. Dominic was one of those spoilt, untouchable kids, that life generally gave an easy ride. The private school he went to trained them to be arrogant and self-assured. Clifthill College had after all, during its illustrious history, produced three prime ministers, many members of

Parliament, military leaders, and a sprinkling of African dictators.

Dominic flung the gunk into the builder's bag.

"It's only dead weed and stuff!" Dominic laughed.

"Thanks." Edison said flatly.

"Although some do say that Bob Soup might have been thrown in there," Dominic leered. "To disappear."

"That's rubbish." Edison replied.

"The 'Moser's' could have ate him, and then pooped him out!" Dominic joked.

He picked up a suspicious looking smelly brown clump of weed and threw it in Edison's direction.

"Watch out!" Dominic shouted "Dino dregs, incoming!"

Edison jumped out of the way as the missile just missed him and landed, splat on the wooden planks. The whole gangway rocked and swayed as Edison regained his footing.

"Stop it Dominic!" Edison growled.

"Just a joke Eddie." Dominic grinned back.

Reg looked over, alerted by the commotion.

"Dominic!" Reg shouted. "I'm watching you lad!"

Dominic sheepishly went back to clearing out his dirty bucket, but when Edison looked over to him a bit later, he found Dominic staring daggers back at him.

Edison was leaning slightly over the gantry, pulling up another heavy bucket of slime, when he felt something knock into his shoulder. Before he knew it, he started to slip towards the edge of the gantry, instinctively making a grab for the wooden handrail. It was too late and his wet rubber clad fingers couldn't grip the slippery rail. His gloves squeaked as they rubbed along the wet surface. For an instant everything went into slow motion. His brain told him that there must be a way to hold on, to grab something, and not fall off the safety of the platform.

He started to tumble into the tank of murky water below. Before he knew it his head was plunged underwater into a swirl of foaming bubbles. He felt little pockets of air fizz about his face, and drift up through his hair. His rubber gloves started to swell and become heavy as they filled with cold water. His hearing became muted as liquid started to enter his ears. All sound now distant and muffled under the surface. He could just hear the murmur of panicked voices above, and the hum of the water pumps deep below. How long he sank for he couldn't be sure. It felt like years, as his young life, sped by in a sequence of images and scenes. His thoughts confused and panicked. It was as if one part of his mind was experiencing the drowning, while another part was somewhere else watching it all unfold.

Soon he felt his body begin to lift and float upwards towards the shiny underside of the water. He opened his mouth and gasped for breath as his head cleared the surface. Dirty cold water stung his eyes and he found it hard to focus on anything. The shouts and screaming had got louder, and he could just make out the blurry shapes of the keepers running about in panic.

As his eyes cleared a little, he saw Reg Green's thick arm reaching out to him, holding a long metal pole.

"Grab hold Ed!" Reg shouted. "We'll pull you out."

Edison made a grab for the pole, but it slipped through his engorged rubber fingers. He started to rip off the rubber gloves, sinking back under the water as he did so. Freeing his hands he started to tread water again, very grateful that he had learnt to swim a few years ago. Staying afloat he reached again for the pole as Reg swung it across toward him.

Out of the corner of his eye he caught sight of a large fin as it surfaced the foaming water. His heart started to thump faster. Even though the prehistoric creature was just a few feet away, he also knew it was safely caged behind thick security glass. Something deep down though, his natural instinct perhaps, just produced more panic. He started finding it hard to breathe and worried that at any moment his lungs would fill with the tanks dirty water.

The Mosasaur was just feet away. Its large crocodilian head was wide open, showing a mass of its sharp, meat eating, teeth. It looked so close, really close. The creature thumped itself into the glass wall, its interest only on the boy thrashing about in the water in front of it.

Edison made another frantic grab for the pole. Above him Reg shouted orders to the other keepers but Edison couldn't make out what they were all saying.

Something brushed against his leg below the water. It felt rough and heavy. Panic again rushed through his body and he reached urgently toward the pole, frantically treading water. With relief he caught hold of its hooked end with both hands. He kicked his feet, propelling himself toward Reg, and the safety of the gangway. Behind him he felt something sharp catch at his foot. He kicked as hard as he could against it and felt his feet connect with something solid. A sharp pain ran up his leg. Had he kicked the side of the wall and broken an ankle?

"Quickly Ed!" Reg shouted, there was now real panic in his voice.

It was then that Edison realised that something was wrong, very wrong. He looked across to his right and saw one of the divers banging urgently on the glass. The diver was on the other side of the glass to him. Edison had thought that he had fallen into one of the empty tanks, ready for cleaning. Instead he had fallen into one of the aquariums smaller holding tanks. And this tank was occupied by one of the prehistoric carnivores.

Edison panicked and again lost hold of the pole, his head slipping below the water. He swallowed a large gulp of murky bitter liquid. He could see blood swirling in the water, emanating from his ankle. In front, hovering just below him, he caught sight of a marine dinosaur's large grey silhouette. It was a Ichthyosaurus, and its dolphin like body looked ready to launch another attack.

Edison propelled himself up, and as his head cleared the surface, he spat out a mouthful of the evil tasting water. Reg reached down with his huge arms and heaved Edison out of the tank, dropping him roughly onto the gantry.

Reg turned quickly and smashed the metal pole against the head of the pursuing Ichthyosaurus. The creature had broken the surface, its huge mouth open and bloody. The pole struck the creatures head firmly and bounced off. It was enough to make it change course and dive back under the water. The metal pole flew across the tank, struck a wall and sank.

Edison lay exhausted, his heart thumping madly.

"He's injured!" Reg shouted.

Edison looked up at Reg and then down at his own ankle. It was covered in blood and Edison could see jagged teeth marks torn into his flesh. Blood was pumping quickly out of the injuries onto the platform. He now realised how close he had come to being eaten.

Reg took off his T-shirt and wrapped it around Edison's left leg, applying pressure to the wound. He pushed down firmly, hoping to stem the flow of blood, making Edison wince.

"Keep calm lad," Reg said. "There's an ambulance on the way."

Edison watched as the make shift bandage started to turn red with his blood.

A worried huddle of keepers had gathered around. Edison could see Dominic, looking horrified, in amongst them.

“Does it feel broken Ed?” Reg asked.

“I don't think so. I'm not sure.” He replied.

"Will he be OK?" Dominic cried his voice wobbly.

“Take off your T-shirt!” Reg shouted back.

The world began spinning and Edison started feeling really dizzy and nauseous, and perhaps Reg somehow realised this. He took Dominic's T-shirt and used it to raise Edison's injured leg slightly as he repositioned Edison onto his side, in the recovery position.

Edison could now see through the wooden slats of the walkway down to the tank below. He saw his own blood drip from the platform and dissipate into the aquarium water. He would never be sure, and it may just have been the confusion of the accident, but he thought that he could see, in the murky water below, the face of the Ichthyosaurus, floating just below the surface of the water, hungrily watching him.

He looked up at Reg, his face drawn and frightened. His body felt so cold and he shivered uncontrollably. Reg continued to apply pressure to his wound but Edison couldn't feel it anymore. All the pain had leaked away. A soft mist had started to blur his vision. A deep maroon fog crept in, encircled, and then totally engulfed him. Everything went very still and silent.

Chapter 21
Hospital.

Mandy sat in the hospitals waiting room on an uncomfortable plastic orange chair, part of a row that ran down the side of the room. Well thumbed and dog-eared magazines littered small tables positioned randomly between the seats. The quiet room smelt of bleach and other cleaning chemicals, and for some reason the heating was turned fully on. The room felt small and oppressive, cocooned in the airless heat. She would have liked to open a window, but these were all sealed shut.

She was worried about Edison and the rooms smell was starting to make her nauseous. She had accepted a cup of coffee from Reg Green from a coin operated drinks machine in the corner of the room. Reg looked just as concerned as Mandy when he passed the cup of coffee over to her.

"Bit hot." Mandy said as she tentatively took a tiny sip from the rim of the thin plastic cup. She put the hot cup of coffee down onto the table next to her seat, to let it cool.

"It tastes horrible too," Reg apologised. "Sorry."

A series of sterile machines beeped and flashed in the corner of the private hospital room. His bandaged leg lay uncovered sticking out from under the bed sheet.

"Oh Ed," Mandy said, cupping his hand and sitting down next to the bed. "What happened love?"

Edison stirred and opened his eyes.

"Hi Mum," A tear glinted in his eye. "Sorry."

"Hey, don't worry. It was an accident." Mandy squeezed Edison's hand gently between her own. "You're going to be fine."

"I fell into the water." Edison explained. "I nearly got eaten!"

"It's OK. You're safe now." Mandy comforted him. "The doctor has said that you can go home later today."

"My leg?" Edison reached down to feel the thick coarse bandage wrapped tightly around his limb. "It's not broken." Mandy explained. "The bite wasn't too deep, it will heal."

Edison looked worried.

"Can I walk?" He asked.

"Yes, of course you can!" His mum smiled. "You'll just limp about the place for a while."

Before, while sleeping, Edison had a vivid flashback of the incident in the aquarium. His head was immersed under the water and the marine dinosaur thumped itself against his leg. He hadn't felt it bite him, at all, but remembered seeing the blood as the keepers pulled him out.

"It's not a major wound. We gave it really good clean and a few stitches." The doctor had appeared beside the bed. "You'll have to rest it, give it a chance to heal."

"Thank you doctor." Mandy said.

The doctor held up an X-ray of Edison's leg.

"You had a lucky escape Edison." The doctor explained. "The dinosaur's teeth missed all of your main arteries and didn't crack the bone."

"Thanks." Edison said, examining the X-ray closely.

"Thankfully your friend Reg administered excellent first aid."

The doctor gestured towards the corridor. Reg stood behind a glass window and waved, a huge smile of relief on his face. Edison raised a hand and slowly waved back, his whole body felt stiff and ached.

"That's the first dinosaur wound I have ever treated." The Doctor said. "I can't wait to tell my kids tonight!"

He then took Edison's hand and shook it firmly, smiling.

"Good to meet you Edison." He said, giving him the X-ray as a keepsake as he left.

"Thanks Doctor." Edison smiled.

The doctor casually waved and walked off down the ward to visit his other patients. Edison was sure that none of these would have dinosaur wounds.

#

Reg gave Edison and Mandy a lift back to the flat later that day. He usually drove one of the zoo vans or jeeps and today they were all sitting upfront in his beloved Land Rover. The dashboard inside was messy as the zoo vehicles tended to get used by various members of staff, who rarely cleaned them. Empty crisp packets and food wrappers filled the glove compartment and covered the vans floor.

“Thanks Reg.” Mandy said, inspecting the interior. ”Nice, err, car.”

“Apologies, the zoo vehicles do sometimes get into a bit of a muddle.” Reg explained a little embarrassed.

There had been a group of journalists and cameramen waiting outside the hospital when they left. A life threatening accident, at the world’s only Dinosaur zoo, was news. A dinosaur story involving a child nearly getting eaten was really *big* news!

Camera lights illuminated the hospital foyer and flashed brightly as Edison was pushed out of the building in a wheelchair, sandwiched between Mandy and Reg. Reporters shouted questions, but Edison couldn't tell what they were all saying, above the loud mash of voices. Reg helped him out of the wheelchair and up into the jeep quickly. The hospitals public relations representative had read a short statement to the press about the accident. She said there would be a longer one from Dr. Harriet May over the coming days. The press of course wanted answers now. How had the boy fallen into the dinosaur tank? Was it an accident? Who had saved the plucky boy? Would Edison lose his leg? Where were the boys parents when all this happened? Was it even legal to employ a child of thirteen in a Dinosaur zoo? The questions kept on coming.

Reg just smiled good naturally when the reporters bombarded him with their questions. He said nothing apart from the occasional ‘no comment’, and started the vans engine.

When they drove up to the flat they were greeted by more reporters, huddled like gnomes on the front lawn. The trio managed to push their way through the hubbub, Edison using a crutch with one arm and Reg supporting him with the other. They got into the front door without having to say anything to the press.

"I'll put the kettle on." Mandy said.

Edison and Reg flopped down into the sofa. The day had been traumatic for both of them. It felt as if all of their energy had drained away.

"Sorry Ed," Reg apologised. "I should have been there to stop it happening.”

Edison wanted to tell Reg what he thought may have happened. He just wasn’t sure how to tell him, as he knew Reg wouldn’t like it.

“Tea,” Mandy said coming back into the room. “And biscuits.”

“Thanks Mandy.” Reg smiled.

“Milk for you,” Mandy said to Edison. “You need the calcium.”

The three drank their drinks and ate their biscuits in silence. Edison and Reg both dunked the digestives into their mugs. Outside a reporter started to knock at the front door, but they all ignored him.

#

That afternoon they all stayed inside the flat, the reporters buzzing about outside. Edison gave Reg a guided tour of his bedroom. He wanted to show him all of his dinosaur memorabilia, and he really hoped that Reg would like his room.

"Amazing!" Reg said, as they entered.

Reg ran around the room like an excited schoolboy, picking up books, investigating the wallpaper and looking at the drawings on the wall. He played with the plastic dinosaurs, flicked through the books and generally getting excited. Edison's room really was a shrine to everything dinosaur.

"What an amazing room!" Reg repeated. "I *dreamed* of having a room like this when I was your age."

This was the first time anyone had ever said that his bedroom was amazing and Edison glowed with appreciation. Alex had always said his dinosaurs were stupid, and Mum complained that everything was all so hard to clean. Even Orla wasn't that fussed about all of his stuff.

Edison sat on his bed and suddenly felt emotionally overwhelmed. He almost thought he would start to cry, and he certainly didn't want to do that in front of Reg. He felt a small tear start to form in the corner of his eye, so pretended to be engrossed in a book. It must have been the stress of the accident catching up on him, he thought. He had come very close to death after all. He suddenly thought of his dad, his *real* dad. Where had he gone? And why? He thought that it was about time that his Mum told him the details. Edison didn’t want to die before knowing who he was.

Reg was investigating the dinosaurs on the bookshelves and hadn't noticed Edison sitting quietly.

"Oh, I always wanted one of these!" Reg said, lifting up an illuminated Stegosaurus and showing it to Edison.

"You OK Ed?" Reg asked.

Edison looked up from his book. Why wasn't his Dad still around? And why couldn't Alex have been a bit more like Reg?

Reg sat down on the bed next to Edison and put one of his huge arms around his shoulder. Edison almost collapsed, he felt so weak and tired.

"Reg, you know the accident?" Edison murmured.

“Yes?” Reg asked kindly.

"Well,” Edison paused, “I think I was pushed."

The two sat in silence and Edison felt safe and warm with Reg’s arm around him.

“Don’t worry about that now lad.” Reg said comforting him.

Edison didn't even notice himself drifting off to sleep.

Chapter 22
Home.

There was the sound of laughter coming from downstairs. Edison heard his Mums unusually happy giggle, which automatically made him smile. Bright sunlight shone through the bedroom curtains as he sat up in bed. He must have slept for at least ten hours. The accident had totally exhausted him and his whole body felt bruised. He opened the curtains and looked out into the tidy back garden. The lone totem pole stared back at him. He couldn't wait for that stupid thing to be chopped down. The sooner the chainsaw cut it up into tiny bits the better.

He embarrassingly remembered last night when he had nearly started crying in front of Reg. His leg really ached from the dinosaur bite and his head felt muggy. The bandage was also making his injury feel really itchy. He gave it a quick rub but disappointingly couldn't quite get to the source of the itch. Perhaps a wooden spoon from the kitchen would reach down to scratch it. He quickly put on some clean clothes and limped downstairs.

In the living room his Mum was drinking tea and laughing at a story Reg had been telling. Edison didn't think that he had seen her laugh like this for years.

"Alright Ed?" Reg asked, as Edison hopped into the room. "I was telling your Mum about Bob Soup. You know, about his toe replacement finger."

His Mum cracked up, spraying tea across the room. The story had her in stitches. They both looked over at Edison and tried to suppress their laughter.

"Have I been asleep long?" Edison asked.

"Long enough to become famous!" Reg said, pointing to the television.

The sound was mute, but the news showed pictures of Edison, the Dinosaur zoo and the accident. There was even an animated 're-creation' in the top right hand corner of the screen. Mum and Reg were watching two rolling news channels at once, the second of which was a smaller screen within the larger.

The animated film showed a distinctly strange looking computer generated dinosaur attacking an even odder CGI boy, battling it out in the zoos aquarium! The animation was stiff and crude, and had obviously been churned out quickly for the news item.

"It wasn't like that!" Edison shouted, angrily pointing to the TV.

Both Reg and his Mum couldn't stop themselves from bursting out laughing again.

"You wait until you see what other things they are coming up with love." His Mum said smiling.

"There's already a toy doll of you!" Reg said. "It has a detachable leg apparently, although you have to buy the dinosaur toy separately."

“I'll get you one for Christmas.” His Mum joked.

"That's crazy!" Edison exclaimed, shocked.

"Look outside love," His Mum laughed. "That's really crazy."

Edison went over to the window and peered out through the closed curtains. It was still very sunny and Edison had to squint to see outside. On the pavement in front of the flat was a mass of people. Reporters, cameramen, well wishers with flowers and handmade 'Get Well' banners, a hotchpotch of neighbours and general 'nosey parkers' all huddled together outside.

The road was blocked with television outside broadcast vans and police cars, keeping the peace, and even an industrious ice cream van had set up shop. A queue of onlookers waited patiently in line for their celebratory 'dinosaur' cones and prehistoric shaped lollies. The dinosaur cone was an extra large '99' type, with chocolate dinosaur shapes instead of the sticks, and strawberry jam flavour sauce liberally squeezed over the top of it.

Edison drew the curtains quickly and turned to his Mum and Reg, speechless. He really couldn't think of a thing to say. The whole situation was so surreal. Reg broke the silence.

"Bob Soup never got this kind of media attention when he had his finger bitten off!" He said seriously, causing his Mum to fall off the sofa in hysterics!

#

Orla had popped over to see how Edison was. She had no option but to squeeze her way through the crowd milling about outside.

"Delivery coming through. Out of the way please." She shouted, pushing by the gawping strangers and carrying a small bunch of flowers.

"Is Edison a friend of yours, Miss?" A reporter cheekily shouted out to her as she knocked on the flats door.

Orla turned to sternly face him and then smiled.

"No, he's my boyfriend!" She shouted mischievously.

The crowd let out a collective 'Ooh' and the reporters started to furiously take pictures and scribble in their notebooks.

Orla happily posed for the cameras before the door opened slightly and Edison pulled her inside of the flat. They stood in the hallway with Orla laughing her head off.

"What are you doing?" Edison asked her seriously.

"Just mucking about." Orla laughed. "Anyway how are you Ed?"

'No, he's my boyfriend!' Echoed loudly from the television screen in the next room. The 'live' news was beginning to transmit the footage of Orla from only seconds before.

"Ooh," Shouted his Mum from the living room. "Is that true, love?"

"No!" Edison shouted back.

“Hello Mrs Hope.” Orla giggled, as they both walked into the room.

#

The rest of the day was spent in the flat, holed up like prisoners. The crowd waiting outside never seemed to get any smaller and if anything it might have grown. The home telephone had been taken off the hook, as it had been ringing continually. Thankfully the reporters hadn’t got hold of any of their mobile phone numbers, so they could contact and speak to their concerned relatives and friends. Edison had been chatting to his Granny Nell and Granddad Roy telling them he was OK and that the news was exaggerating everything, and no, he didn’t have a girlfriend.

“I always said it was dangerous working with dinosaurs.” Orla said.

Edison could have exaggerated his heroism during the whole incident, of how he had battled with the creature and fought it off. But he knew Orla wouldn’t believe him.

“It wasn’t my fault Orla.” Edison replied.

"You could have just got a pet,” Orla argued, “A cat wouldn’t kill you!"

“What about a lion?” Edison replied. “A lion would…”

"OK." Orla admitted.

Edison smiled smugly and folded his arms.

“But only an idiot would have one as a pet!” Orla shouted.

The TV news was screening their animated re-creation of the whole zoo attack again, and Orla laughed like a hyena, watching the computer generated figure of Edison swimming frantically, yet stiffly, away from a giant plastic looking Ichthyosaurus.

“You look more like a movie star on the telly.” She teased him.

“Funny.” Edison smiled blankly.

“No worries!” Orla chirped.

“Orla, it’s serious, I think I was pushed into the aquarium,” Edison explained, looking at Orla. “By Dominic White!”

"Even Dominic isn’t that stupid.” Orla replied.

“Well I felt someone shove me in the back.” Edison stated.

#

When a stupid radio disc-jockey unsympathetically turned up at the flat, dressed in a dinosaur costume, but actually looking more like a tubby Godzilla, Reg suggested that they all slip away. The overweight DJ had wanted Edison to do some voice spots for his daily radio show. Mandy sent him away with a flea in his ear, calling him a ‘talentless twit’. The sight of the humiliated man, fleeing the scene, dressed as a huge lizard became another news item that night. The DJ tried to laugh the whole incident off, but the public viewed him as an even bigger idiot then they had previously.

"You get going," Mandy said to Edison and Reg. “I’ll stay here and keep them busy.”

"Thanks Mum." Edison said, kissing his Mum on the cheek.

“See you later Mandy.” Reg waved. “Ed will be safe with me.”

“I know Reg. You’ve saved him once already.” Mandy smiled. “I’ll go upstairs and create a distraction.”

Edison, Orla and Reg left Mandy holding the fort and sneaked out of the back door of the flat via the kitchen. There was an emergency fire escape built at the back of the flats. Edison had to be careful of his leg down the narrow metal staircase, but his limp wasn't too bad. They avoided the reporters by leaving via a dirt track that ran behind bushes in the garden.

What they sadly missed was Mandy throwing a bowl of cold water out of her bedroom window onto the fancy dressed DJ waiting patiently below. The crowd let out a collective roar of appreciation as the wet, overweight, Godzilla waddled off in shame to his radio car.

"Where are we going then Reg?" Edison asked.

"There's a place I know." Reg replied. "I don't think anyone will find you there."

They had taken a canvas bag full of food, snacks and drinks and as the afternoon sun started to set, it almost felt like they were all off for a picnic.

It was still warm and the atmosphere golden as the group walked away from the streets and up over the Downs. Reg seemed to be leading them towards the zoo. It was only when Edison realised that the route was very familiar to him that he saw that they were actually heading towards the area where his secret tree stood.

"I want to show you somewhere I used to go when I was a lad." Reg explained.

Edison wanted to say something, but kept quiet. Could they really be going to the same place?

"It may have changed a bit," Reg said. "I haven't been there for many years. It's a good place to sit and think."

"At least we'll be away from those stupid reporters." Orla said.

It wasn't long before they arrived at the clearing, not far from Edison's secret oak tree. The tree that he had climbed to gaze down on the zoo. He hadn't been here for ages; he hadn't needed to, now that he actually worked inside the zoo.

"There's an excellent view from up there." Reg said pointing up at the tree. "You can see right across the whole zoo!"

Edison was excited to know that Reg had also climbed this tree in his youth. Perhaps Reg too had his childhood daydreams, of working at the original zoo, hidden amongst the leaves, at the top of the tree.

"When your leg gets better we'll all have to climb it." Orla said to Edison happily, grabbing his hand for a brief moment. Her hand felt so soft and warm, and a spark of excitement ran down the back of his neck. There was nothing he would like more than to spend more time with Orla. Showing her the view from inside the top of the tree and telling her his zoo stories.

Edison smiled back, he supposed now that he worked at the zoo, it didn't matter anymore whether his lookout was a secret or not.

The three of them sat at the base of the tree and Orla laid out the food and drinks that they had brought with them. They sat in silence with their make shift picnic, admiring the amazing sunset starting to form over the city. Edison was about to tell them both about how he already knew about the tree, and the close encounter he had with the pterodactyl, when Orla broke the silence.

"Edison thinks he was pushed into the water Mr. Green." Orla said.

"Orla!" Edison exclaimed, surprised at her telling Reg.

"I know." Reg said.

Reg explained that Edison had told him as much the night before when they got home from the hospital.

"I don't know for sure if I was pushed or not." Edison said, glaring at Orla.

"It's something that needs to be looked into." Reg said thoughtfully, eating his sandwich.

Orla looked triumphantly back over at Edison.

The reds and oranges of the sunset warmed their skin making it glow. Halo's of golden light shone around the rims of the trees. Small insects and pollen flitted about in the shafts of light coming through the leaves. The city was peaceful, and but for a blackbird singing loudly in the tree canopy, and the distant sound of happy children playing football on The Downs, all was calm.

"Tomorrow," Reg said. "I'm going to inspect The Water World CCTV footage."

Edison and Orla looked seriously at Reg.

"Then we will have the answer."

Chapter 23
The Darkness of the night.

Edison awoke with a start from a comfortably and deeply immersing dream. It was a few years into the future and he was an assistant keeper at the zoo. Aged about 19 he worked at the zoo full time, apart from two days apprenticeship training at a local college. He also seemed to be romantically involved with Orla. They had been out on a date, when something interrupted his happy sleep.

His bedroom was dark, lit only by a couple of his dinosaur lamps. The large khaki stegosaurus was giving off the brighter light and that side of the room emitted an eerie green glow. It was as if a small alien space craft had landed in the corner and settled on the bookcase, deciding that this was the perfect place to invade.

The room was deadly quiet and Edison wasn't sure what had woken him. He looked at his bedside clock and saw it was 2.20am, in the morning. It was the middle of night and he couldn't hear any noise coming from outside. At first he thought he had been woken by Alex returning home. He remembered the times his Step-dad had returned to the flat in the past, drunk and waking the whole neighbourhood with his terrible singing. But Alex hadn't been at the flat for weeks.

Edison was now back at school, the summer holidays over. His leg was much better and for the first few days back at school he was a bit of a hero. The news reports had died down but many of his school mates couldn't wait to hear his story of falling into the Dinosaur tank and nearly getting eaten.

Reg had told him that it *was* Dominic who had pushed him into the aquarium. Whether it was accidental, or a deliberate and nasty act, wasn't clear. The authorities were investigating, but there were differing accounts of the whole incident. The police were taking statements and looking at the CCTV footage. Dominic's dad had apparently hired an expensive lawyer, so nothing was going to happen fast. Dr. Harriet May had dismissed Dominic and hired the zoo's own equally expensive legal help. She had visited Edison at home to apologies and repeatedly stated that she would fix things.

Reg reckoned that the marine dinosaur's injury had probably been the creature's first 'investigative' bite. It was using its mouth to see what tasty morsel the keepers had dropped into its world. Edison would easily have lost his foot, leg or even died, if the creature had taken a proper bite out of him.

Edison sat up, concentrated and listened hard, but couldn't hear anything unusual. There wasn't even much traffic sound at this time of night. The city was asleep. His bedroom was silent and still. He looked over at the clock again. The last time he had been up this early was the night he had followed Alex into the zoo. The night of the burglary. The night Alex vanished.

Suddenly he heard a scraping sound coming from the bedroom window. The curtains were closed, so he couldn't see outside, but it definitely seemed to be coming from that area. For a brief moment he wondered if one of Orla's cats was outside sitting on his window sill, tapping the glass with its paw, trying to get in. But that was a crazy notion. Why would one of her cats be outside his window? He yawned and rubbed the sleep out of his eyes.

Tap, tap, tap.

Edison jumped; something was knocking against the glass.

He remembered an occasion when the buildings TV aerial cable had become unattached in a storm, and swung down from the roof. It slapped itself against the building all night in the wind. Had the cable become dislodged again?

Edison pulled back his duvet cover and tiptoed over to the window. He looked at the drawn curtains and hesitated about opening them. This was stupid, he thought. It's only the cable again, swinging in the wind. He took a deep breath and pulled the curtains apart as fast as he could.

The first thing he saw was the ugly head of the last remaining totem pole standing sentinel in the garden. The badly painted wooden face stared inexpressively back at him. The sooner that ruddy thing was chopped down the better, he thought. The garden was dark and misty, lit only by the roads amber street-lighting. The grey mist hovered silently over the lawn, blanketing the whole garden. Shafts of orange street-lighting penetrated the gloom, slipping through the leaves of trees that surrounded the area. The mist made the night seem frozen, like a photograph. Edison could tell it must be cold outside as he felt chilled standing here in his pyjamas. Summer really was now over.

A fox darted across the lawn cutting a swirling trail through the mist. The creature paused for a moment, sniffed the air, and then quickly darted beneath a bush and disappeared. Had the fox woken him? He remembered hearing their eerie cries in the past, sounding like the ghosts of abandoned babies, haunting the night. Their calls far worse than most of the zoo's dinosaurs. He hadn't heard any foxes since waking up, and if anything the one he had just seen looked pretty spooked itself.

The mist settled and filled the space where the fox had once been. A small movement caught Edison's eye and he looked down. Something had moved in the garden below. He rested his forehead on the cold glass and looked down as far as he could, over the windows edge. Instantly he yelped and jumped back with fright. Standing in the swirling mist was a huge man with a heavily scarred face, looking up at him.

Edison couldn't quite believe what he had just seen. Who was it standing there? Why were they standing there? His legs began to shake and felt wobbly and weak. It was as if his feet had suddenly turned into heavy concrete blocks, pinning him to the bedroom carpet. His whole body was frozen in fear.

Edison knew that he had to look again. He used all of his mental energy to convince his body to move and stepped toward the window. Slowly he put his head against the glass and looked down into the garden. No one was there. The man had gone.

For an instant Edison wondered if he could have imagined it. But the man's face had been too hideous to be imagined. Scabby sores and deep red scars, cut across the man's skin. The details of the disfigured face had become etched into Edison's mind in an instant. One of the staring eyes seemed to be white and sightless, with a pink scar slashed across its middle. It looked as if the man had recently been in a freak accident with a threshing machine or industrial cheese grater. Something violent had slashed and gashed, deeply into his skin.

Edison unlatched the window and carefully opened it. Cold night air began to stream into the bedroom through the gap. Edison slowly leaned his head out, peering over the windows parapet, but couldn't see anything. The garden was quiet and empty. The man, if he had existed, was nowhere to be seen. Edison stretched himself out further, gripping onto the window frame, and looking down the side of the building. The metal fire escape was deserted. It was then that Edison noticed a small window, on the floor directly below him, was wide open. It was their kitchen window.

A terrible, bone chilling scream, erupted from downstairs.

It was his Mum, she was in trouble.

Chapter 24
Home Invasion.

Edison bounded down the stairs in panic, his Mum still screaming in the living room. The door was open and as he dived through he was met by a terrible scene. His mum sat cowering on the sofa and a huge figure loomed threateningly over her.

"Mum?" Edison shouted.

The hulking figure turned to face him.

"Hello, *hero!*" The man shouted sarcastically. The scars on his face opened and closed, mirroring his mouth, as he spat out the words. Edison could see his mouth was also missing a few teeth. Broken stumps projected from his raw gums. The man grinned evilly at them.

It was then that Edison realised who the intruder was. It was the stranger he had talked to at the zoo days before the break in. The same man who he had seen pursuing Alex through the zoo on the night of the robbery.

"Where's your step-dad?" The man asked.

"Sorry?" Edison replied, genuinely confused.

"Where's Alex!" The man shouted angrily.

Both Edison and Mandy were dumb-stuck and silent. Alex hadn't been at the flat for weeks. What had he done to make this man so angry? Had Alex caused the damage to the man's face? It seemed unlikely, Alex was a coward, and Edison had seen him running away from the stranger.

"He's.." Mandy began to explain.

"He's not home yet." Edison interrupted.

Mandy looked over at her son, confused. Edison continued looking up at the huge man.

"He should be back soon." Edison lied.

"That's good," The huge man stated bluntly. "Because I'm here to kill the bloody thief!"

#

Reg Green had been wandering around the ransacked house for most of the evening. Dr Harriet had asked him to look around once more inside Bob Soups house, to search for any clues to his disappearance. She had hinted that the stolen contents of the safe may be somewhere in the house. Reg really didn't believe that Bob had anything to do with the break in at the zoo. The man had always seemed honest and reliable and had worked at the zoo for years. It didn't make sense.

The robbery seemed so long ago now, what with Edison's terrible accident in the zoo's aquarium and the ensuing publicity. The police didn't seem that interested anymore and it was only really Dr Harriet that seemed keen for answers.

"I know Bob is a trusted colleague Reg." Dr Harriet had told him. "But even you must admit that it's very suspicious that he disappeared right around the time of the break in?"

Reg didn't want to believe it, but of course it was odd. He wasn't that close to Bob, but the man seemed friendly enough and worked hard at the zoo. Seeing his house trashed like this did make the whole affair even stranger. Who had ransacked his home? It didn't seem like a simple burglary, the flat-screen TV was still on the wall, and there was an expensive music system sitting untouched beneath it. This seemed more like someone had been desperately searching for something particular. Maybe Dr Harriet was right and others also thought that the contents of the safe were inside Soups house?

It was getting really late and Reg needed some sleep, the comfort of his bed was calling him. He clambered over a ripped and overturned sofa, its upholstery spewing out over the carpet. He guessed that he wouldn't find anything now. Whoever had smashed the place up had probably found what they wanted. He decided that he would report the incident to the police. He would however leave it until the following day, it wasn't that urgent. The police knew that the zoo had access to Bob's home and had been asked to be informed of any developments. Well this, he guessed, was a development, but it could wait.

As he picked up the telephone Reg noticed a piece of notepaper on the floor near one of the table's legs. This hadn't been there last week when he visited the house. Perhaps who ever had ransacked the place had disturbed it; maybe it had fallen out of one of the many overturned cupboard drawers tipped out across the room.

Reg picked it up and saw that there was a bloody fingerprint and a few handwritten names and numbers. Two names stood out, SOUP and ALEX, both scrawled in block capitals. The number beside the name Alex looked familiar. Reg tapped it into the telephone keypad and heard the familiar dialling tone. It rang for a little while and then clicked into the female voice of an automated recorded message.

"Sorry the number you are dialling is unavailable. Please try again later." Beep. The line went dead.

Reg put down the phone and looked again at the number.

The only Alex he could think of was Edison's step-dad, who had also mysteriously gone missing. Reg opened his mobile phone and searched for Mandy and Edison's home number. A cold chill ran down his spine as he realised the number written on the paper was the same as that in his mobiles address book. He rang the number, this time from his mobile, but there was still no answer.

Reg ran out of the house towards his parked land rover, as fast as he could, and before the automated lady had even finished her message.

#

"I found this." The stranger held up a battered key card. It was the same one Edison had stolen from the zoo for Alex.

"Now Mr. Soup has vanished, perhaps gone to ground?" The man said looking at the photograph on the security pass. "I can't find him anywhere."

"I don't really know him," Edison replied. "I know he went missing."

"Well, Mr. Soup was useful to me." The stranger explained. "He provided me with the details of the zoo's security, the CCTV cameras and the code to get in."

"I wouldn't know." Edison replied.

"Really?" said the man. "Interesting."

Edison tried to remain as calm as possible but he could feel his legs shaking. There must be a way to save his Mum and get this terrible man out of their flat. He could see that the house phone had been ripped out of its wall socket, and his own mobile was upstairs in his bedroom, so calling the police wasn't an option.

"Now Mr. Soup, Bob, didn't give me this key card." The man said still, holding the pass as if it where a dead rat hanging between his fingers. "So I can only assume that he was also helping someone else break into the zoo? That someone being your idiot Step-dad, Alex."

"Alex?" Mandy asked nervously from the sofa.

"I looked around Bob's house." The man continued, ignoring Mandy.

"Tore it to bits, but didn't find a thing."

"I don't think Alex even knows a Bob Soup." Mandy said. "Does he Ed?"

Edison looked at his Mum but didn't have time to explain.

"And then I saw you on the news!" The stranger continued, staring at Edison, an evil smile on his scarred face. "Your accident was very popular."

The man explained how he had been recuperating inside his flat, staying away from people, while his injuries started to heal. He hadn't even been able to contact his client to claim his final payment. The goods had been stolen by Alex. Never in his career had a job gone so badly wrong. The man had a reputation to uphold, he told them. There was no way he would go back to his client empty handed, no way.

He couldn't visit a hospital, his injuries were too suspicious, so he had treated himself. Army life had trained him well for such circumstances. The D.I.Y patch up job on his face had worked pretty well, hadn't it?

Edison and Mandy had no choice but to listen. The man was obviously crazy as well as dangerous. His face looked horrendous, like something out of a horror film.

"I recognised you as the nosey lad I'd met inside the zoo." The stranger continued. "At first I wasn't that interested. 'Stupid kid', I thought, falling into a tank full of dinosaurs, 'What an idiot!'"

Edison shuffled awkwardly on the spot. How much more did the man know?

"Lucky that you didn't get eaten!" The man grinned nastily.

"It was an accident!" Mandy shouted protectively, but the man wasn't really listening.

"I have been spending some of my recuperation hacking into the police computers. I was looking for the thieves and lowlife of Clifthill. The kind of local scumbag I might have happened to bump into, one stormy night inside the zoo.

Edison stood his ground, unemotionally listening to the man's story. He couldn't let him know that he too had been in the zoo that night.

"Anyway I chanced upon some photos in their missing persons files, and there he was, Alex, reported missing." The man said. "I recognised him immediately."

"Alex?" Mandy asked. "Alex didn't break into the zoo. Edison?"

Edison looked over at his Mum but didn't give anything away. It would be dangerous for her to know anything about Alex's involvement in the robbery. He hoped that the man would be less likely to harm her if she seemed genuinely ignorant of the whole matter.

"I had to wait a while, for my injuries to heal, and for the hubbub outside your flat to die down." The man explained looking at Edison.

"But I have been watching, waiting and so far haven't seen Alex. Therefore he is either here, laying low, or somewhere else, hiding."

"We haven't seen him!" Mandy blurted out.

"Mum!" Edison yelled.

"What I *do* know is that either you," The man pointed nastily at Edison, "Or your mother, must know where he is, and the whereabouts of the rucksack, which he stole off me."

"He hasn't been home for weeks." Mandy cried.

Edison looked over at his Mum, pleading with his eyes for her to keep quiet.

The man walked ominously towards Edison.

"So where is Alex? Where is my rucksack?"

#

Reg drove the land rover as fast as the old girl would go across the centre of town. Bob Soups house and Edison's flat were on opposite sides of the city. Thankfully at this time of night the roads were empty with only the occasional taxi driving about. The mist was thick and the poor visibility made Reg drive slower than he would have liked. He had to get to the flat as soon as possible, something in his gut told him that The Hopes might be in danger. He pressed the redial button on his mobile phone but the same automated message clicked onto the line. Why weren't Edison or Mandy picking up their telephone? He threw the phone down into the passenger seat next to him, annoyed, and continued driving towards the flat.

#

Mandy suddenly jumped off the couch. She had to protect her son and rescue them from this terrible situation. While the man was distracted talking to Edison she picked up a heavy wooden carved elephant off the floor, which they often used it as a door stop. It was the last remaining carved figure made by Alex still left in the flat. Mandy had kept it as it was useful, but also because it one of his only carvings that looked like the animal it depicted. She wouldn't have said that it was a good sculpture, but it did actually resemble an elephant!

She gripped the carving as hard as she could and smashed the solid chunk of wood violently into the back of the man's head. Sadly it was like hitting a grizzly bear with a beach pebble, it simply bounced off the stranger's solid skull. The huge man turned around, surprised and growling. As he turned, only slightly dazed, he deliberately flung his arm out in a wide arc and smashed his fist, like a medieval mace, into Mandy's chest. The impact forced all of the air out of her body, and lifted her up off her feet. She flew backwards into the air. Edison stood stunned as his Mum crashed down unconscious into the sofa.

"Stupid cow!" shouted the stranger. He started walking threateningly towards her fallen body.

"Mum!" Edison cried out, but she lay frozen to the sofa. At least he could see from her chest movements that she was still breathing. The force of the man's blow must have temporarily knocked her out.

Edison had to get this man away from his Mum as soon as possible and out of the flat.

"It's outside!" Edison shouted. "Alex hid it in the garden."

Chapter 25
The Totem.

Edison wasn't sure what he was going to do next. He knew that by lying to the man he was only going to make him angrier, but he had to get him out of the flat, and away from his Mum. Perhaps he would get the chance to lock the man outside? He could then run back in and get his mobile to call the police. It might work.

As the two of them walked into the misty back garden the stranger kept a tight grip of Edison's arm and shoved him along.

"Don't think of trying to run." The man explained. He wasn't going to let the lad escape, not until he had his rucksack back.

Edison pointed to the nine foot totem pole Alex had carved. It stood at a slight angle, projecting out of the grass.

"It's hidden up there." Edison told the man. "Alex stashed the rucksack at the top."

"What the hell is it?" The man asked, looking up at the badly carved totem pole. He could just about recognise a human head carved out of the wood and what looked like a winged bird.

"Alex made it." Edison told the man blankly. "It's a Totem."

They both stared up at the brutally carved and amateurishly painted totem pole.

"What that piece of shit?" The man asked. "The thing looks cursed."

Edison could tell that even though the huge man had just the one healthy working eye, it at least had excellent vision.

Edison knew that if the man let go of him he could climb the totem in an instant. He was used to climbing his Oak tree and even though Alex may have been no artist he had at least conveniently provided many parts on the sculpture to hang onto. Edison guessed that the huge stranger would have no way of following him if he did get to ascend the pole.

"So my rucksack is hidden up there?" The man pointed to the top of the totem.

"The top comes off and there's a secret hiding place hollowed out on the inside." Edison lied. This was all fantasy of course. As far as he was aware Alex hadn't dug a hollow into the top of the totem and he doubted it would come off. The whole thing was rickety, for sure, so bits had fallen off, but this was by accident rather than design.

"Ingenious." The stranger said. He genuinely seemed surprised and paused to think for a moment.

“So I suppose you want me to let you go and climb the thing?” He asked Edison.

“It won’t take me long.” Edison replied. He had already decided that as soon as the man let go of his arm he would spring up the totem pole, jump from the top into the bushes, and flee. He would be back inside the flat and locking the door before the stranger even had a chance to chase him. It was a risky plan, but Edison didn’t have any others.

“OK.” The man said. ”But I’m watching. Don’t try anything stupid.”

Edison felt the man’s grip on his arm release, now was his chance. He bounded toward the totem and grabbed hold of its thick trunk. In a moment he was off the ground, his hands reaching out for something to grab hold of and pull himself up with.

“Slow down!” The man shouted bluntly.

Edison turned to look and saw the stranger staring smugly back at him. He held something shiny and metallic in his huge right hand. It was a gun, and it was pointed straight at Edison.

“Like I said, don’t try anything funny kid.” The man’s scarred face grinned nastily.

#

Mandy woke up lying on the sofa not knowing where she was. Had she fallen asleep in front of the television? She wasn’t sure. The room was quiet and empty. The TV was turned off and her body felt cold.

She suddenly jerked and panicked as she remembered the huge stranger. Where was he? Where was Edison?

Both her hands felt sore and in pain. When she moved them she found that they were clasped together, bound with sticky tape. Mandy eased herself uncomfortably upright so that she was in a sitting position on the sofa. The stranger hadn't tied up her feet, or bound her mouth, that was something.

Mandy could see the telephone laying on the floor. It was the type with the keys on the handset. If she could just plug it back into the wall socket somehow, she might be able to dial out. It didn't look broken.

She tipped herself onto the floor as carefully as she could, her elbows breaking the short fall on to the carpet. She started to crawl towards the telephone on her knees pushing the handset towards the wall, the lead dragging behind. With some difficulty she was able to manipulate the small white lead back into the wall socket. It was fiddly, with both her hands stuck together, and she kept dropping the end, but eventually it snapped into place. The telephone came to life with its familiar and comforting dialling tone.

Mandy clumsily tapped in the numbers 999, congratulating herself for at least buying a handset with chunky keys.

The number seemed to ring for ages.

"Emergency. Which service please?" The operator said, coming onto the line. Mandy could almost have cried with relief.

"Police!" Mandy whispered down the line. "Please, I need the police."

#

Edison held on tightly to the painted surface of the rough wood, perched high at the top of the totem. He balanced his feet on a couple of carved wings that Alex had inserted into a section of the bird-like head. Edison guessed that this was based on an American Indian depiction of an eagle, but Alex's version looked more like a diseased owl.

Edison looked down at the stranger and saw the glint of the gun, its barrel still pointing up at him. The only thing Edison could do was pretend to search for the stolen rucksack. He started feeling about the top of the totem, looking as if he was searching for something hidden, but really hoping to dislodge a piece. A chunk of heavy wood might make a good weapon.

He knew that he could still jump from the totem and across into the bushes, but would he miss getting hit by a bullet if the man used the gun? It was a risk, but he didn't seem to have any other options.

"Get a move on!" The huge man shouted out below.

A car was revving its engine loudly somewhere on the road outside the flats. Edison hoped that this would be the small distraction he needed. He looked back down at the stranger, enveloped in the mist, hoping that he would be looking towards the road. He wasn't.

"Don't worry kid. Just a joyrider." The man said looking up at him. "You just find me the rucksack."

The stranger was well aware that Edison might be trying to find a way to evade him.

From where he was, high up in the air, Edison caught a glimpse of light approaching on the other side of the flats. A narrow driveway ran down one side of the block and the mist here seemed lighter. The noisy car had been steadily getting closer and suddenly the driveway filled with blinding white headlights. A battered Land Rover rocketed down the passageway, its noisy engine echoing off the sites of the building. It was as if a fiery dragon had decided to fly into the garden. A plastic wheelie bin got caught against the cars bumper and rose into the air. It clattered into a wall, its contents thrown widely.

Edison looked down at the huge stranger, who was now looking surprised at the approaching car. Caught off guard the man shielded his eyes against the bright headlights. He staggered back away from the totem pole, blindly aiming his gun in the direction of the light. He fired. A loud burst of gunfire rebounded around the garden.

The Land Rover accelerated and careered over a set of shallow steps that led down to the lawn. It propelled itself into the air heading directly for Edison and the totem pole. Edison breathed deeply and jumped. He jumped as hard, and as far, as he could. The heavy metal bonnet of the four wheel smashed into the base of the wooden pole and wrapped itself around. The noise was tremendous as the Land Rovers radiator exploded into steam and the totem pole split like a matchstick.

Time slowed as Edison flew through the air, away from the falling totem, and towards a large rhododendron bush. He watched as the familiar figure of Reg fell out of the driver's side of the damaged car and rolled across the grass. The huge stranger had momentarily stopped and turned to look as the heavy totem fell towards him. He jumped aside but was too late. The bulk of the dense wooden trunk smashed into his chest, felling him, and nearly cutting him clean in half. His dying hand fired one last aimless shot as the totem crushed him. Edison saw the guns muzzle flare and felt something speed past his head. The stray bullet had just missed hitting him.

Edison fell into the wet leaves and abundant flowers of the thick bush and bounced. He instantly thought of lumberjacks and their warning cry of 'Timber!'

After finding his way out of the tangled bush he rushed over to see if Reg was alright. The head keeper had simply jumped up and wiped mud off his jeans.

"Well that's the end of my lovely 'Landy'" He remarked, looking sadly at the mangled car.

Reg looked down at Edison and put his hand comfortingly on his shoulder.

"Bit of a close shave there Ed, wasn't it?"

They both sat down on the grass and Edison tried not to think about the dead body crushed under the fallen totem pole just a few feet away. Together they watched the steam rise from the mangled car and listened to the sound of distant sirens getting ever closer.

Epilogue

The next few days were filled with news reports and the press camping outside, yet again, on the Hope's doorstep. Edison, Reg and The zoo were featured heavily on the television news and in the newspapers. 'Mystery of the night stalker', 'zoo hero escapes- again!' and 'Totally Totem-ed!' were headlines on news stands across the country.

The coroner and police forensic team had to wait for the fire brigade to release the lifeless body. Using special winches and lifting equipment they pulled the totem up off the dead man, before they could drag the flattened corpse out. It had almost been cut in two, with the blood stained clothing mostly holding it together.

All attempts to identify the body had failed. No one was sure who the dead man was. No fingerprint or dental records existed to name him. In interviews Edison and Reg had both confirmed that it was the same man who had visited the zoo days before the break in. Police Detective Williams confirmed this by matching the zoo CCTV footage against photographs of the corpse. Blood found on a fire extinguisher inside the burgled office matched the dead mans. Although the man's face was badly scarred it was obviously him. The coroner had asked a veterinarian colleague to confirm that the multitude of scars on the dead mans face may have been inflicted by an animal of some kind. It remained unknown as to how the stranger had received these injuries or the exact animal involved.

Edison had an idea that the man might have received the injuries from a pack of the dinosaurs. He looked at Reg and could see that he too shared a similar notion. Neither of them told the police about this. The zoo really didn't need any more damaging publicity.

The police told them that they were now very concerned about the whereabouts of Alex and the keeper Bob Soup. Seeing as the dead man was armed and dangerous there was a real likely-hood that he may have been involved in their disappearance.

Edison told the police about Alex breaking into the zoo, but kept quiet about everything else that he knew.

"He wanted a rucksack Alex had taken." Edison told them. "Something he had stolen from the zoo."

If they had known that he had given Alex the old key-card and also been in the zoo that night, it wouldn't have helped them solve the mystery of who the dead man was. But it would mean that he would be likely to lose his job at the zoo, and he wasn't going to let that happen. Edison didn't exactly lie to them, he just didn't tell them all he knew or suspected.

Dr. Harriet May told the police about the series of telephone calls she had received since the robbery, offering to sell her back the stolen contents of the safe. So far she had been unsuccessful in testing the validity of these, and to whether the callers really had the goods. She rewarded Edison and Reg for their courage by holding a small party at the zoo. Edison's recent accident in the aquarium and his survival from the mysterious stranger moved her greatly. The party was a small celebration for staff, family and friends. A select group of the press and a local TV news team was also invited, to help put a positive spin on things.

In different rooms, and in different parts of the country, both Alex and Bob Soup saw the story unfold on the TV news channels. Bob was hidden away in a London flat, at Huge Foods expense. He wasn't sure what his options were now, but felt that he would be looked after.

Alex sat in a cheap Bed and Breakfast in Cornwall, wondering what to do next. He had tried contacting the zoo director, but so far she had seemed uninterested, or unable to trust him, about him having the stolen items from the safe. At some point Alex would have to surface, and he even considered returning to the flat in Clifthill; the stolen cash wasn't going to last for ever.

The news had even reached Jacobi in his hotel suite in Chicago via a BBC news cable channel. He had guessed who the dead man might be, as the Fixer had still not replied to any of his emails. Why the man had been targeting a boy who worked at the zoo, and his family, he had no idea? It all seemed very strange and something he would subtly look into, once Bob Black allowed him to go back to London. His plan to start farming dinosaurs for their meat would have to be put on hold for a little longer.

Detective Williams still had no idea as to the identity of the dead man, but he did have some idea as to why the man broke into the zoo. He had an insider at the zoo who had recently been working for them undercover. The man had now gone missing, but the Detective knew that he was OK. They had advised the man to disappear soon after the break in. He had been passing knowledge to a major Food company at their request. A company that Detective Williams and his team very much wanted to investigate.

The Detectives mobile phone rang.

"Hello?" He answered.

"Hi it's Bob, Bob Soup. I've got some news."

THE END

Acknowledgements

Kaja May for correcting the many drafts of this book, being a constant support, and excited proof reader.

Taro for your happy laughter, play and inspiration.

Mum for being a great Mum and a lifelong source of wisdom, love and encouragement.

Dad for being one of the most natural storytellers I have ever known.

Pete Avery, Miki Cash and Jaime Pardo for their friendship, support, creativity, and senses of humour.

Helen Brunsdon and Andy Wyatt and their lovely family.

Bristol zoo - My local zoo, I took some ideas from you and am a big fan.

4:2:2 Bristol for giving me my first proper job after leaving college. Aardman Animations for many years of excellent training in animation and story telling, and having faith in some of my hair brained children's series ideas. Picasso Pictures for giving me my first opportunity as a commercials director. Green Ginger puppet studios for opening my eyes to a totally different world of story telling.

Chester for leading me on all the fun and inspiring walks.

Thank you for reading this book. I would love to hear from you at my Amazon page or on my website www.dinosaurzoo.co.uk

Author

Nick Mackie is an award winning animator and director. 'Edison and the Dinosaur zoo' is his first novel. As a creative he previously worked for many years at the Oscar winning Aardman Animations studio, won BBC Talent, a Royal Television Society award, and developed a couple of preschool television ideas. His short films have been in competition at various international film festivals including Annecy, Portland, Edinburgh, London and others.

For the last couple of years Nick has been concentrating on his writing projects, illustrated books, and a smattering of animation thrown in. At the moment he is working on a new illustrated children's book and developing an idea for a preschool television series. He hopes to start writing the next Edison Dinosaur book very soon.

Nick lives in the South West of England with his fiancée, young son and their border terrier.

Author Notes:

When I was a young kid one of the most exciting things happened. John Craven, off the telly, came to Bexhill-on-sea, my home town, to film a report for 'Newsround'. Newly discovered Dinosaur footprints had been uncovered on the beach! The tides had weathered away the soft rock revealing them. The beach at Bexhill can change a lot, with stormy seas uncovering new groups of rocks and washing away others.

Sadly I was at school that day and first heard about it from my Dad, who had gone down there and to get Mr Cravens autograph (which I still have). That night at teatime I was so excited, having this precious autograph and imagining the prehistoric dinosaurs uncovered down on the beach.

As a typical boy I was a big dinosaur fan. My bedroom had a huge vividly coloured poster of a giant T-Rex, its mouth bloody, full of ripped flesh, as it pinned down a smaller creature - A classic design and the stuff of nightmares.

Dad took me and my siblings down to the beach to see the Dinosaur footprints, and to be honest, I was unimpressed. My childhood imagination had been working over time and I think I was expecting to see actual dinosaurs or their bones at the very least.

What I saw was a row of classic dinosaur footprints, three toed, large, and sunken into the sandy rock. The footprints where probably those of an Iguanodon, or a Megalosaur. The tides eventually covered them up or washed them away. The beach still turns up a footprint at low tide every now and then.

One day I will track down that episode of Newsround, to refresh my memory. Maybe the local paper from that date will even have a picture of John Craven standing on the beach, pointing and looking in awe?

This book is a novel, a story. I apologise if I cause palaeontologists and dinosaur experts to tear out their hair. I have done research, but will inevitably get things wrong, or deliberately alter facts to fit the story. But let's face it; you guys have been changing the Dinosaur story yourself over the years. I miss the leathery Brontosaurus! I know it's still there, but now it's an Apatosaurus - One day you will probably cover it in feathers!

I hope you enjoy the book,

N. R. Mackie 2012

www.dinosaurzoo.co.uk